The Ninth Session

Deborah Serani

Relax. Read. Repeat.

THE NINTH SESSION
By Deborah Serani
Published by TouchPoint Press
Brookland, AR 72417
www.touchpointpress.com

Copyright © 2019 Deborah Serani
All rights reserved.

ISBN-10: 1-946920-75-4
ISBN-13: 978-1-946920-75-1

Editor: Kimberly Coghlan
Cover Design: Colbie Myles, ColbieMyles.net

Connect with the author at www.drdeborahserani.com

First Edition

Library of Congress Control Number:2019948594

Printed in the United States of America.

For Ira

"All of us are much more human than otherwise."

—Harry Stack Sullivan, Psychoanalyst

Session One

Monday, June 5

The light slowly filtered in from the other room as I opened the door. This was the last moment of the unknown, where two strangers meet and a life story begins.

Most times, I've no idea which seat in the waiting room a new patient will choose. Sometimes, though, I can make a good guess from the initial phone call. Usually, the depressed patient, feeling weak with fatigue, sits in the first seat available, whereas the anxious person, eager to feel relief, selects the seat closest to the consultation room.

Not that it really matters. There are only six chairs in my waiting room.

"Mr. Ferro?" I rolled my neck around the waiting room. Then checked my watch. *Eight o'clock on the dot.*

Seeing no one, I pressed my lips together.

Did I make the appointment for eight or eight fifteen?

I left the door ajar, walked to my desk, and re-checked my schedule. I slid my finger down the Monday, June 5th grid in my appointment book to the eight o'clock hour, and there was his name: Lucas Ferro. He'd be my last appointment of the night.

Okay, it's for eight o'clock.

Maybe he's running late.

While I waited, I reviewed my notes from my telephone conversation with Ferro. I opened the crisp manila file and heard a shuffling, then a sputtering hiss of air in the waiting room. I turned toward the sound, unsure of what it was.

A magazine falling on the floor?
The air conditioning shutting off?

I listened for another moment or two and, hearing nothing more, went back to my desk.

My office suite was a beautiful setting and one I didn't mind spending so many hours in. The waiting room, a spacious rectangle, was lined with several Ficus trees and exotic plants, paintings from local artists, and burled wood furniture contemporary in design. The thickly upholstered leather chairs were caramel in color, and the teal-flecked carpet stretched from wall to wall. The vaulted ceiling housed three skylights, flooding the room with an abundance of natural light.

My consultation office was just as large, and there was ample room for my desk, two chairs, and the proverbial psychoanalyst's couch—and of course, an etched nameplate on the door: Alicia Reese, Ph.D. Psychologist.

Across from the built-in bookcase was a long picture window overlooking Oyster Bay. At this time of night, the evening sunset gleamed across the water, layering the inlet with a silvery orange hue.

I turned my attention back to the Ferro file, and I heard it again.

Thumping movements.
Hissing sounds of air.

Then silence.

"What *is* that?" I asked aloud with growing curiosity.

I'd been working in this building fifteen years and knew all its creaks, thuds, and mechanical whirrs. But I couldn't decipher these sounds. They weren't familiar.

I tapped my pocket, confirming the presence of my panic remote. In all the years I'd been in practice, I never found a need to use it.

I got up from my desk and moved toward the door that led to the waiting room. An emerging sense of uneasiness took hold. I heard a hollow voice say something I couldn't catch and then trail off.

I jolted forward, took out the panic alarm, and held my thumb on the button, ready to send the signal. I entered the waiting room but saw no one.

Again it happened. The bang of something hitting the ground. Then a rush of air.

I focused my vision on the sounds, turning my gaze toward the far-right corner of the reception room.

The darkened bathroom.

I walked in willed steps toward the nearly closed door. Drawing in a deep breath, I opened it all the way with a poke of my index finger.

There, standing against the corner wall, was the shadow of Lucas Ferro having a panic attack.

"The tile...it's cool," Ferro said, breathing raggedly like a drowning swimmer. *Hissing sounds of air.*

"It's okay, Mr. Ferro." I followed his frenzied movements with my eyes. "I'm gonna step away and give you some room."

I flicked on the bathroom light as I moved away. As the room brightened, I saw Ferro's face. It was sweaty and chalk white. His black hair flopped in wet patches across his forehead, and his eyes were narrow slits of blue. His body moved in spasms, halting and then starting again.

Ferro tugged at his shirt collar as he drew in rapid breaths. Watching him, I felt the anxiety leave my body and the return of my clinical posture. This was a crisis, and I went into crisis mode.

"I want you to listen to my voice as you take in a deep, slow breath."

Ferro lifted his shoulders, straightening himself from the stooped position against the wall. His knees bent several times as if unable to bear his own weight. Then, all at once, his body buckled toward the sink, but he anchored his two hands on the porcelain base to steady himself. As he drew in a series of deep breaths and huffed them coarsely through his mouth, his feet wobbled and slapped the tiled floor.

Thumping movements.

"You're doing great," I said. "You're gonna be just fine."

Soon, color began to return to his face.

"I want you to slow your breathing even more. Like this." I modeled the technique for him.

Ferro followed my instructions and formed a slower breathing pattern, ending the hyperventilation that gripped him. Bit by bit, he raised himself to a solid standing posture. A self-conscious impulse took over as he saw his reflection in the mirror. Ferro slicked back his hair with his fingers, smoothed his clothing, and blotted the sweat from his face with a swipe of his arm. Then he smiled at me weakly.

The crisis was over.

As he found his way back from this acute attack, I realized there was no longer a need for me to be holding the panic alarm. I tucked it back into my pocket. I waited for what I thought was a good moment to ask my very first question.

"Can you move out of the bathroom?"

Ferro nodded his head and walked toward the reception area. Upon moving into the waiting room, his eyes sought my approval to sit down.

"Yes, of course," I said.

He slumped into the chair and tilted his head back against the wall. I moved a few seats away and waited for him to find a sense of balance.

In the long stretch of silence that followed, I studied him in sidelong glances, trying not to be obvious. He was young, probably mid-to-late twenties, and his dark blue eyes glowed with intensity. He was dressed in a green and white Abercrombie & Fitch shirt. There was a moose logo on the left chest pocket. His slacks were washed in a dark tan hue, and he wore no socks with his deck shoes. On his wrist, a flash of gold—a watch with chunky links. He was vulnerable right now, but as the panic faded, I noticed he was muscular in build. And tall. Six feet or more.

We remained quiet in the room for a while. I was always good with silence. It was a comfortable experience.

"I'm worried you won't be able to help me," Ferro said finally. His voice was dry, cracking slightly.

"What makes you say that?"

He was silent as he regarded me. I wasn't sure if he was trying to find the right words or still seized by panic. The silence stretched as he continued looking at the ceiling, occasionally rubbing his hands over his eyes and face. He cleared his throat several times, fighting the dryness.

"Let me get you some water," I said, getting up. I filled a paper cup with cold tap water in the bathroom.

Ferro drank it down in one large gulp. He crumpled the cup and rolled the shapeless form between his hand and fingers.

"Been in therapy before. Nothing's helped," he spoke again.

"But you're here tonight. Something made you feel hopeful."

Ferro said nothing but shifted restlessly in his seat. I gave him a few moments before leaning forward to talk again. Just then, he stopped moving altogether and turned his gaze toward me. It was a searching look, and at that instant, it was as if he was seeing me for the first time.

"I guess... I'm hoping you *can* help me."

"How about we move into my office?"

A beat later, Ferro nodded.

Wanting him to find a level of comfort, I avoided unnecessary words or actions as he made his way into the consultation room. He walked and sat in a nearby chair. He drew in a few deep breaths trying to get comfortable, but it felt like he could take flight at any moment—leaving the session altogether.

"I'm not exactly sure where to begin."

"Why don't you tell me how long you've had these attacks?" It seemed a good starting point.

"About two years."

My eyes widened. "A long time."

"Yeah," Ferro replied.

"Any idea why they happen?"

"It's –uh—it's complicated."

"Complications are my specialty."

Ferro laughed and sat back a little further in his chair.

"Tell me about your work with Dr. Karne," I asked, giving him another place to start. Dr. Paula Karne was a well-regarded psychologist who practiced cognitive behavior therapy in Great Neck.

"Saw her for a few months, y'know, trying to stop the anxiety."

"What kinds of things did you work on?"

"Changing how I think, replacing bad habits with better ones. Stuff like that."

"I see."

Cognitive behavior therapy focuses on in-the-moment issues and how to change them to find greater well-being. Though I worked differently than Dr. Karne, my goal would be the same: to help the patient feel better.

Ferro cleared his throat and spoke again. "I wasn't always totally honest with her, though."

"How do you mean?"

"Didn't exactly tell her what was really bothering me. Thought I'd just go there and learn how to control things. That's all I really wanted anyway."

"To control the panic on your own," I said, reframing his thoughts.

"Yeah. But I know I gotta be more open. That's why I decided to try again."

"Being honest is important in therapy."

Silence came down like a curtain, and we lingered in its folds for a while.

"Why do you think it was hard to be more open with Dr. Karne?" I asked him.

"Well, she doesn't really work like that."

"True," I eased back in my seat. "She works just with the behaviors you have. She doesn't get into the nitty gritty things like emotions, memories."

Ferro nodded in agreement.

"Well, what's honesty mean to you?" I asked when it was clear he wasn't going to speak again.

"Showing all the cards, I guess. Talking about things I don't wanna share."

"And feeling things."

Ferro nodded. "Makes me feel weak."

"How so?"

"I really don't like needing other people."

"Dependency makes you feel weak?"

"Yeah."

"Have there been times in the past where needing others wasn't easy?" This was a gentle probe to move him deeper into his thoughts. Ferro said nothing, shutting down by looking away. Sensing I might be moving too quickly, I shifted my approach. "We can talk about those kinds of things at a later time."

"It's hard to just open up to someone you meet."

"I get that."

Keeping track of time, I checked the clock on the end table where Ferro sat. The session was nearing its end. So much occurred and yet so little was done to obtain a formal clinical interview.

"We have just a few more minutes. How about scheduling another appointment?"

"Uh, okay," he said, handing me the shapeless cup.

I took it from him, wondering why he hadn't placed it in the trashcan himself.

"How about seeing me on Wednesday?"

"Twice a week?"

"Actually, I was thinking three times a week."

Ferro glanced out the window and then raised his eyes to mine. As he did this, he shrugged his shoulders. "All right."

"We'll look at why you're feeling anxiety, explore your early childhood, your connections to others."

Ferro nodded.

"Do you know much about Psychoanalysis?"

"A little. Dr. Karne talked about it."

"We're going to explore your thoughts, feelings, and behaviors, but in a deeper way."

"The unconscious."

"Yes," I said, pleased he was familiar with the term. "These techniques will help us kick your anxiety to the curb."

"I'd like that."

"How does seven o'clock work for you?"

Ferro nodded.

I picked up a pen and filled in the Wednesday, June 7th slot. Taking an appointment card from the holder on my desk, I completed his name, the time, and the date. His eyes seemed glued to my every movement.

"Here you go," I said as I held out the card. "We have to stop for now."

"That's it, then?"

"For now."

The arc of the session went from one extreme to the other. Lucas Ferro walked into my office at his worst and left seemingly in control.

"See you Wednesday, Dr. Reese." Ferro paused, looked at me, and extended his hand.

Many classical analysts hold back from any form of touch in sessions. I was a modern analyst, and incidental touch wasn't something taboo to me.

"See you Wednesday," I said and met his hand with my own.

His grip was firm and tight.

Notes

Lucas Ferro, white male, mid 20's. Tall, muscular, well-dressed, and groomed. Presents as cooperative, alert, verbal and intelligent.

Unsure of presenting problem because patient had full blown panic attack before appointment started. Takes up most of the session - so no formal intake done.

Treatment focused on triage and crisis management. Patient is stabilized by the time session ends.

Previous therapist Dr. Paula Karne. Need to get signed release to speak with her. Recommending multiple sessions as week for patient.

Transference: Positive, but guarded.

Counter-transference: Positive. Kicked up my maternal instincts. Worried about his level of comfort.

Relevant issues: I felt significant feelings of dread, eeriness before sessions started. Took panic alarm out. Gave me his paper cup to throw out. What's that about? Is it something symbolic or just a fleeting disregard of noticing where the trashcan was? Feeling exhausted after the session.

Diagnosis: Deferred, but considering Panic Disorder or other anxiety related disturbances. Need to rule out depressive disorders as well.

Prognosis: Deferred at this point. No real clinical data to consider.

Monday Night

The elevator groaned slowly three floors to down to the ground level, and I listened to my heels echo on the marble lobby floor. I liked how the sound clicked above and below me as I walked.

It was a warm, humid day so the ride home would be the same as the one to work—convertible top down. I left the building and got in the car as Steve, the security guard, waved to me from his truck. I tooted the horn as I rolled away, feeling the thick air float across my face and through my long hair as I hit the gas.

The way home took me down the tony thoroughfare of Route 107 in Brookville. As a young girl, I loved seeing the mansions and sprawling estates along the highway when I went boating as a kid in Oyster Bay. I dreamed of living there one day, and while it wasn't a surprise to family and friends when I moved there—finding a crumbling barn and fixing it up with was. The house itself was a carriage house in the 1900's, part of a family-owned, multi-acre horse farm. Years later, the property was subdivided, and Ryan, my husband, and I bought it when we were in graduate school and moved in just after we married. It wasn't a big house, only 1800 square feet, and the parcel of land was considerably smaller than the other homes in the neighborhood. But what it lacked in sheer size was overshadowed by its charm. It took a few years to restore it, but was a labor of love. We kept the original beams and studs, which were visible throughout the house, and the interior was painted a copper white patina. With an open floor plan and an overlooking loft, it was spacious yet cozy. Ryan and I filled it with eclectic things, mixing century's old with millennium's new. We lived in it almost a decade before he got sick.

As I veered off to the private road to the house, the squeaky peeps of the frogs and trills of the katydids lulled me into a peaceful ease. I tried to stay in the moment and not think of Ryan, but by the time I reached the driveway, my eyes blinked back tears. I listened to the gravel pebbles lining the driveway move, clack and shift under the car tires and reminded myself how important it was to dwell in small things since Ryan died. The smell of the morning air, the feel of the wind, and the sound of the night creatures—and now the sound of rocks against rubber. Sensory experiences. Life affirming moments.

I parked the car in the unattached garage and walked into the house through the side door. For a moment, I regarded the house, its space, and its sounds like a sentry guard as I disarmed the security alarm. Deciding I'd be in for the night, I reset it and clunked my belongings onto the floor. My cat, Elvis, a black tabby, bounded out from a corner.

"Hello there, mister," I said, as he pirouetted around my feet.

He followed as I walked to the front door and collected the scattered mail on the floor and as I moved to the bedroom. I placed the stack on my bedroom dresser, along with the rest of the week's mail, undressed, and checked the answering machine.

"This is operator 2416 with a relay call for Alicia. Hi sis. Haven't heard from you. Call me. Nicole."

Beep.

"Hey, it's Mary. Wanted to know if you're going to the psych association luncheon next month. Gary, Charlie, Manny, and Robin are going. David and Denise are a definite too. Give me call and let me know."

Beep.

"Alicia, it's Chris. We're watching "*School of Rock*" tonight. Wanna join us?"

Beep.

I didn't hear the rest of the messages as I changed into a pair of flannel shorts and pulled on one of Ryan's T-shirts. I tuned them out as I did most nights, promising myself that come the morning, I'd call them all back. I threw my hair up in tousled ponytail while Elvis continued to snake around my legs.

"Hungry, huh?" I said to him. "Me too."

I scooped Elvis, walked into the kitchen, and gave him a bowl of water and a can of his favorite salmon mix. Then I brewed some tea and toasted a day-old corn muffin. I sat down in the kitchen chair and let Elvis jump up, waiting for him to coil alongside me after he devoured his evening meal.

I ate in silence as I did most nights now. The only sounds were the humming of the refrigerator and the ticking of the clock. Sounds that reminded me of my childhood home. Where thrums, clinks, and other rhythmic sounds made feel safe.

I was the only hearing member of my family, a Coda—a child of Deaf adults. My dad, Carl, was born Deaf, as was my mother, Vivienne. My parents met at Mill Neck Manor School of the Deaf where they worked—my dad as a teacher of the Deaf, and my mom was the bookkeeper for the school. After a few years of marriage, my sister, Nicole, was born, and she was Deaf too.

When I entered the picture, life didn't change in a drastic way for my family. As a hearing baby, my first words were in American Sign Language, or ASL as it's been shortened to—and I signed long before I ever spoke a word. But as I got older, I went to hearing schools instead of Deaf schools—and learned to speak, just like any other hearing kid did. We were like an ordinary family. Talking, sharing, fighting, and laughing—except in sign. It was a loving home, where touch was a frequent form of communication, and busy hands signed in expressive ways.

But since Ryan died, the house was a soundless place. As a child of Deaf parents, a Coda, silence was always a companion of sorts for me. It never made me feel alone or afraid. It was a comforting space. But this stillness was a heavy haze of loss and grief. Of death and endings.

Wanting to head off the mounting despair, I hiked my shoulders back and rose from the chair. Elvis bolted away.

"Time for *House*," I said to him as I turned off the lights and headed for the bedroom.

Looking over my shoulder, I saw Elvis crouch down, his tail arching and bristling in the shadows. "What is it?"

Elvis let out a slow throaty growl. His ears twitched as he skulked into the darkness.

"Okay," I said as I heard him play with some of his toys.

I grabbed the remote on my way to the bed, slipped into the sheets, and turned on channel thirty-eight. I heard Elvis again as my head hit the pillow. This time, his cry was louder. He hissed several times, racing up the hallway and then back with lightning speed. Then he began caterwauling.

"Damn it, Elvis."

I plunked the remote on the nightstand and flipped the covers off. I walked down the hallway, leveling my eyes for a quick once over in the darkness and found him perched near the window in the living room.

"Okay, buddy. Come with me."

Elvis stiffened as I picked him up and pressed his front paws against me. All at once, he clawed deeply into my skin and batted my face.

"Hey." I yelled and dropped him to the floor. I winced as the caterwauling started again.

Stupid cat, I thought to myself.

I moved into a pool of light to get a look at Elvis' handiwork but felt my heart squeeze tight and then stop dead a beat.

Outside the window was a long, black sedan in the apron of my driveway. Its lights were off, and smoke rose from the exhaust. A flush of heat rushed to my cheeks when I parted the blinds to get a better look.

And as I lifted the horizontal slats with my fingertips, the sedan backed up and jetted down the street.

"Who the hell was that," I said as I walked back to bed.

Supervision

Tuesday, June 6

The trip to Manhasset to Dr. Prader's office at the North Shore Medical Center was only fifteen miles from Oyster Bay. The trip always took more than an hour because traffic on Long Island was inevitable—making it one of the worst places to live. I'd usually treat myself to an Americano at the nearby Starbucks when I arrived early but knew that wouldn't be happening today. The Northern State Parkway was more congested than usual, and I was already late for my appointment.

I passed the time in the unavoidable traffic listening to some Miles Davis but couldn't get the vision of the sedan out of my mind.

Why was I thinking about Ferro after that happened? I wondered. I felt this uneasiness before my session with him and again before I saw the car. "Just a coincidence?" I asked aloud.

But as I wove into faster lanes and out of slower ones, I reminded myself how my imagination intensified when Ryan died. It was easy to recall such moments. The times I thought the phone rang only to discover nobody on the line. The moments I swore I saw Ryan in a crowd—or heard his voice echo in the house. Instances when I called the neighbors thinking someone was breaking into the house—only to discover it was just the trees scraping against the windows. Or the times I thought the garbage cans by the curb were kids playing in the street.

In many moments grief clouded my senses. Distorted from fatigue. And as I thought about the sedan in the driveway, I wondered if what I saw was real.

Was the car really there? I wondered.

My thoughts faded as I looped onto Lakeville Road and pulled into the hospital garage. I glanced at my watch and quickly jogged along the pedestrian pathway that led to the hospital's lobby atrium. I zipped through the doors that led to the psychology department's offices and hurried down the hallway.

Dr. Susan Prader was Chief of Psychology at the hospital, but she was also my supervisor. For the last ten years, we had a standing appointment at the same time each week. It was a time I cherished—an experience that was both invigorating and educating.

Psychoanalysts valued clinical supervision more than any other clinicians in the field of psychology. Born alongside Freud's discoveries of the psyche, analytic supervision with an esteemed colleague provided a therapist, like myself, with an extra set of senses. It was a way to broaden, deepen, and enrich the work I did with patients. A way to check-and-balance issues in sessions. Supervision offered profound and unique bond. Part parent. Part sibling. Part colleague and friend.

Though Dr. Prader and I didn't go to the same schools, we had similar clinical experiences. Both of us treated patients from a psychoanalytic perspective. She worked in a hospital setting while I worked in a private practice. And we shared something perhaps even more important—we were both a Coda.

Prader grew up in the outskirts of Washington, DC and was the only child born to Deaf parents. She took to learning with a passion and was a natural leader growing up. By the time she was a teenager, she was a local Deaf advocate. In college, she took part in the groundbreaking *Deaf President Now* march at Gallaudet University and continued lending her spirit in Deaf legislative actions on state and federal levels in graduate school. Her parents thought the field of law would suit her better, but Susan Prader found her niche in psychology. She was fierce and yet gentle, possessing sharp instincts and insight.

"Sorry, I'm late," I signed, entering the office. "How are you?"

She brought her hand to the middle of her chest and signed, "Fine. Fine." Her silver bracelets jangled as she moved her arm back to her side.

Prader was a beautiful woman, tall and elegant. She wore her brown hair shortly cropped, which revealed the gentle angles of her face. Her skin was smooth and flawless, and her eyes were sparkling brown. Only the reading glasses hinted at her age.

"How far along on the clock are we?" I asked, moving to spoken language. It wasn't unusual for Prader and me to interchange speaking and signing. Codas did that often with each other, moving from ASL to Pidgin English to spoken English.

"We've got a half hour," Prader said, closing the office door.

I slid into the empty chair by her desk. Then I waited for her attention and signed, "How was your week?"

"Good, Busy. But I wish Friday was here already," Prader signed with fast hand movements. "You?"

"Yesterday I had a first session with an interesting patient."

Prader picked up a pen and started writing. "What was the presenting problem?" she asked, no longer signing.

"Well, I'm not entirely sure. The patient had a full-blown panic attack, which took up the whole session."

"A most unusual first meeting," Prader said. "Gonna put him on the couch?"

"Not sure. I'll see how the next few sessions go."

Prader guided me with her experience and wisdom but always let me apply the treatment. "So does this patient have a name?"

"l-u-c-a-s," I finger spelled.

I watched Prader as she jotted some notes. In supervision, last names were never used. It was a way of protecting a patient's privacy.

"So, you have this unusual session, little clinical data, can't say too much about this patient—but are bringing him in today," Prader said with a remote, absorbed look. "Something else is going on, right?"

"You're amazing, y'know."

"Yeah, yeah, I'm all-knowing."

"Well, last night, a car pulled in the driveway and stayed there a while. I have a feeling he followed me home."

"You're certain?" she signed with one hand as she continued writing with the other.

"No, I didn't see the driver."

Prader said nothing and peered over her eyeglasses.

"I could be totally wrong, but I got this feeling he was in that car," I said.

"Tell me about this feeling."

"I felt this dread right before our scheduled session. I was spooked before he arrived, I think. So I took out my panic button. Felt it again when I saw the car in the driveway."

Prader grew quiet and sorted her thoughts. "Let's say you're right. It *was* him. If so, you'll have to address things. Boundary crossing is never good."

"I know."

"Now let's say your instincts *aren't* correct. Let's say it's just some lost driver in the driveway. Now your uneasy feelings aren't related to this patient but are something else. Something within *you*."

I stared off for a moment. "No one's in the building besides me at night when I work."

"Go on," Prader encouraged.

"Sometimes I'm nervous at home. Thought I'd get used to it by now."

Prader said nothing, using silence as a tool.

"I've been having flashbacks. Some good—like remembering how Ryan and I met, our wedding, places we traveled. But others aren't so great."

"You met in college, right?"

"Yes. I was a teaching assistant at NYU in an ASL class. Helped students learn the signs as the professor taught. I remember noticing Ryan because he was such a terrible signer. His signs were awkward and sloppy, but there was something so sweet about him." I felt my heart beat heavily. "The day class ended, he asked me out."

"Sweet," she said. "Any others?"

"I was thinking about when Ryan met my parents and my sister. That was such a great day. At first, I thought it'd be hard for him. You know, how some hearing people are when they enter the Deaf world."

Prader smiled and signed, "Afraid. And nervous, yes."

"Right."

"But not your husband?" Prader signed.

"No. Ryan was so warm and funny." I closed my eyes as I gathered more of my thoughts. "But I have other flashes. The green plaster-chipped walls of the hospital. How drawn and thin he looked when Hospice arrived. Seeing him dressed in his suit in the satin-lined coffin. And the friggin' morphine drip that never seemed to work."

"Mmm," Prader said.

"There's more bad than good ones." I hesitated a moment, piecing together a sudden realization. "The car last night—it was a dark, long sedan. Looked like the limousine we sat in when we buried each of our parents."

Prader nodded, seeing the symbolism. "How long ago was that?"

"Mom was October 2014. Buried my Dad six months later. Then a year later, Ryan died."

"Multiple losses. One right after the other." Prader shook her head registering the chain of traumatic events that moved through my life. She paused a moment and offered her interpretation. "These flashbacks could be influencing your reactions."

"I hadn't considered that."

"Yes, well, you need to take this into consideration personally and professionally." Prader leaned forward in her chair. "Important for you to take care yourself. Maybe you should consider referring this patient out," she signed.

I waited a moment before I spoke. "I appreciate your concern, but there's no need to refer Lucas to another therapist."

Prader widened her eyes.

"If he *did* follow me home, I'll address it. I'll set limits." I paused again and looked at my wedding ring. "I do have moments when it's tough, but I wouldn't be working if I felt fragile."

"Alicia, you *are* fragile," Prader said speaking.

"My caseload isn't demanding. And I'm doing all right."

"While that may be true, you should reconsider this case. It might require more than you have within you."

"Well, let's see how things go in the next session."

"Fair enough." Prader glanced at the chrome-plated clock on her desk. "It's time for us to stop today."

"Okay. See you next Tuesday," I signed.

Prader let her head fall forward and softly closed her eyes. Then she brought her index finger up to her lips and extended it outward. "Yes," she signed.

Tuesday Night

By the time I arrived home after supervision, the thoughts of Lucas Ferro and the worries faded from my mind. I peeled off my clothes, slipped into a long t-shirt, and washed away the remains of the day. While I started making dinner for myself, I wondered why Elvis wasn't under my feet, pawing for his food.

"El," I called.

Hearing nothing, I stopped midway of my sandwich-making and looked for him in his bed.

"Elvis?" I said louder.

I stepped into the hallway searching with my eyes. Seeing nothing, I walked into my bedroom and looked in his favorite hiding places. Under the bed. In the shower stall. Beneath the tiny space under Ryan's dresser. He was nowhere to be found.

Knowing Elvis could never resist the sounds of the can opener, I walked back into the kitchen and grabbed a can of food from the cabinet. "C'mon, buddy, chicken and giblets."

Still nothing.

I heard a rapping at the front door and a sudden faint voice.

"Just a minute," I yelled out and ran back to the bedroom to pull on my bathrobe. I ran back to the bedroom and pulled on a bathrobe. I hurried back to the door and placed my eye onto the peephole. As I tried to focus on the figure outside, the doorbell rang.

"Helloooo?"

"Hey, Isaiah," I said, opening the door.

"Elvis has left the building!" he said with a broad smile.

Turning my attention to the cat I said, "So there you are." Elvis wiggled out of Isaiah's arms and bolted into the house.

"Found him in our yard again, Alicia."

"He shimmied the window. Again? But I left it just a couple of inches open."

"Don'tcha think Houdini's a better name for him than Elvis?" Isaiah asked, brushing cat fur from his shirt.

"He *is* a better escape artist than he is a singer. That's for sure."

"Why do you think he's always coming to my house?"

"Well, your house is the place to be," I said, touching his cheek. "Even I like it there."

Isaiah was one of two foster children who lived with Chris and Melanie D'Amico. Together, they owned several Best-Buy franchises in Nassau County and had all the latest media and gaming technology. To say it was a cool place to live was an understatement. It was heaven for kids and tech-geeks alike.

I motioned for Isaiah to come into the kitchen. "I'm making a sandwich. Want one?"

"Nah, I'm not hungry."

"How about another game of Scrabble? I've been holding back on kicking your butt, y'know."

Isaiah considered the offer for a moment. "Nuh-uh. My moms are gonna be lookin' for me. I didn't tell them I was coming here."

"Really? You better head on back."

As Isaiah nodded in agreement, shadows made a way across the street. We caught the shapes simultaneously. It was his mother, Chris, and his foster sister, AJ.

"Uh oh. I'm busted."

Soon, they were at the door.

"I see you have my broken arrow," Chris said.

"Isaiah was just returning Elvis back home. He managed to get out again today," I said hoping to smooth the awkward moment.

She smiled and then narrowed her eyes toward Isaiah. "Saiah, you have to let us know you're leaving the house."

"But...I told AJ," Isaiah fibbed while looking at AJ for support.

"Yeah, uh, you didn't tell me that," AJ replied, sneering playfully at him.

"Thanks, traitor," Isaiah said and ran off to play with Elvis who was up in the loft. Soon AJ followed.

Chris allowed Isaiah and AJ the moment and turned her attention toward me. "You got time for me on your couch, Doc?" Chris laughed.

"Still having trouble with AJ, huh?"

Aurora Jean Sheridan, or AJ as she liked to be called, was an emergency foster care placement. AJ's parents, George and Anita, struggled with heroin addiction—and as they recovered in a local rehab, Child Protective Services relocated AJ with Mel and Chris. I had met AJ several times since she arrived, and she struck me as precocious and street-smart. Her wild, long red hair and mischievous eyes gave her an alluring beauty—making her seem older than her sixteen years. She was a handful, no formal diagnosis needed.

Chris touched her hand to her forehead as if she was suddenly afflicted with fever. "She ran off two nights ago. Got herself a lip-ring in the city. I'm sure that'll go over great at the next court date."

"When's that?"

"Next week," Chris said. "But who knows if she'll still be with us. The judge might just place her in juvenile hall if she can't work with the *no-leave* rule we got going in the house."

I'd been around AJ enough to see she wouldn't be staying with the D'Amico's long. She clearly didn't like being under the direction of anyone else's rules but her own. And it sounded like Chris and Mel were realizing that now too.

"And now this one thinks he can just take off and go anywhere too," Chris said arching her eyebrows toward Isaiah.

"Anything I can do?"

"Thanks, Alicia, but no. Sometimes we can make a difference. Sometimes we can't."

I nodded, agreeing.

Chris yelled out to Isaiah and AJ. "Let's go, guys!"

Within seconds, they hurdled down the stairs.

"I win," Isaiah said, sliding on his knees to the door first.

"Not yet, dweeb," AJ replied, her red curls wild in her face as she ran past him, out the front door, and into a tree along the walkway. "I win," she yelled.

"Enough," Chris said to Isaiah, lifting him from the floor.

"Yes, Ma'am," he said.

"Sorry about the Elvis thing. I really don't know how he was able to get out again," I told Chris.

"No, worries," Chris said as she opened the door to leave.

As they passed over the threshold, I held out my hand and waited for a high-five from Isaiah. He jumped up and smacked it hard.

"G'night guys," I said.

I watched as Chris and Isaiah walked down the steps, arm in arm. Just before they walked onto the street Isaiah asked, "What's a broken arrow, Mom?"

"It's a military term. A broken arrow doesn't fly straight, so the military uses it as a code for a nuclear threat," Chris said, tousling his hair.

"A broken arrow doesn't fly straight? That's tight," AJ said jumping down from a limb. "Can we try that? Shoot a broken arrow?"

"Not on my watch," Chris said as they faded into the night.

I closed the door, locked the bolt, and looked at my own broken arrow, who was now chowing down on his dinner. "You are so totally grounded, mister."

I legged it up the stairs and found the window open just as I'd left it, about two inches wide. No way he'd get out. But the screen was gone, and I saw claw marks on the sill and stray tufts of black fur on the floor. Tell-tale signs Elvis really might have pulled a Houdini.

Maybe he was able to squeeze it open enough to get through it?

I opened the window wider and eyed his escape route. A few small jumps from the roof to the overhanging soffit, and down the gutter.

I slammed the window shut, locked it, and pulled the toggle to the ceiling fan. I watched the string sway back and forth as I walked downstairs.

"Don't even think about it," I said as Elvis crept past me back to the loft.

Session Two

Wednesday, June 7

Ferro said nothing but offered a thin smile as he entered the office. He was more casually dressed today, wearing a red short-sleeved polo shirt and frayed jeans. Again he was sock-less but in sneakers this time.

"How've you been since our last session?" I asked.

"Okay."

"That's good." I watched him take a seat. "So your anxiety level's less today?"

"Yeah. Better. I have a feeling you could really help me."

"Really?"

"Something about you," he said, tossing his car keys on the table next to him. I looked closely and saw an insignia on the key fob but couldn't tell what it was.

"Our first session was rough," he said, swallowing and staring off. "I totally fell apart."

"It was demanding. For both of us, I think."

Ferro looked around the room and then back at me. "You really took care of me. Made me feel safe. And you're easy to talk to."

I said nothing, wanting him to continue.

"That's important for me. To be comfortable."

"To feel safe too," I said, peering again at the key fob.

Ferro followed my gaze with his own eyes. He sensed my preoccupation with the car keys and picked them up. "You drive a Porsche too?"

I cleared my throat, feeling embarrassed. "Actually, I don't. What kind do you have?"

"Boxster," he said. "My baby."

"Nice. Is that the only car you drive?"

Ferro clasped the keys tightly in his hand. "Yeah, why?"

"Well, Lucas, I've been asking each person I work with if they drive a black car." I paused to consider my next sentence. "I saw one in my driveway a few nights ago, and it frightened me."

Ferro stiffened but said nothing.

"It's not unusual for patients to be curious about where their therapist lives," I said, setting up the out if he needed it.

Again, Ferro remained motionless.

"I just need to find out who it is so we can talk about it." I tried to be delicate. "You know, to find out the psychological meaning behind the visit."

Ferro placed the keys in his pocket and leveled his eyes to mine. "I don't own a black car, Dr. Reese. Mine's red."

There was tension in the air for a few moments. My mind wandered to supervision with Prader and how we considered my unsteadiness as coming from within myself. Not from outside sources.

"Okay then." I considered Ferro might feel offended and wanted to spare him any further discomfort. "Hope you can forgive the directness of my question."

"Nah, it's okay."

"Good. I just needed to get that out in the open."

Ferro eased back into his chair. "You see, *this* is what I mean. There's an honesty about you. Makes me feel like I could tell you anything."

I stepped back into the analytic rhythm. "You didn't feel that in therapy before?"

"Not really."

"Well, I'm glad you feel it here." I turned toward my desk and pulled out Ferro's file. "Let's get things started then."

After going over how treatment works, getting a medical history, signing releases, arranging weekly payments, and finding three standing appointment times, we were ready to go.

"Okay, Lucas. Tell me a little about yourself."

"Well, I'm twenty-seven."

My eyes widened, inviting him to speak further.

"Just started working at the *Long Island Tribune.*"

There was a long pause, and I watched as he winced, unable to pull out a conversational thread. "What do you do at the *Tribune*?"

"Staff writer."

I waited to hear more, but Ferro quieted again. I sensed he needed more guidance and structure, so I became more active in the session. "Did you study journalism in college?"

"Yeah. But originally, I was a business major."

"Why the change?"

"Found business really boring."

I shrugged my shoulders. "I never took a business course. So, don't go by me."

"Trust me. It was dull."

"What didn't you like?"

"For starters, I didn't wanna major in it."

I blinked hard and shook my head. "So, how'd that happen?"

"Family business. Family pressure. Rule the kingdom kinda thing."

"What business is your family in?"

"Ice."

"Ice?" I asked.

"King Ice. My great grandfather, Robert Kingston, started it in the early 1900's. We supply ice to places like the Fulton Fish Market, to stores and restaurants in the city and upstate New York. Block ice. Bulk ice. Turbo Ice."

"Turbo ice? Never heard of that."

"Nuggets of ice, for drinks and stuff," Ferro explained. "Ice is big business."

"Is that right?"

"Over fifty million last year."

"Wow. So, why not be part of the kingdom?"

Ferro sighed. "I like spending as much time away from my family as possible. The business wasn't for me. Besides, my brothers are the blue bloods. They run things now."

"I see." I didn't want to go too deep too soon, so I kept the interview light. "So, you ditch business and turn to journalism?"

"Yeah. Sophomore year I took a couple of writing courses. Found I liked them—so I changed my major." He held his gaze and looked at me. "After I graduated, I worked at *The Miami Press* for a while."

"So, what brings you back here to New York? The *Tribune* job?"

"Actually, my mom died." Ferro cleared away a catch in his throat. "This past January."

"Was she ill?"

"No."

"What happened, Lucas?"

"Long story."

"If this isn't a place for long stories, I don't know where else is."

Ferro nodded and lowered his head as if to collect his thoughts. Soon he raised his eyes to mine. "There was an accident in the factory—and my mother died. She was in the wrong place, wrong time. Typical for her."

"What do you mean, typical?"

"My mother was very hands-on in the business. Pushing and controlling everything." His tone was flat, unemotional.

"Where'd she push herself?"

"I'll give you a great example. In the morning, she'd always be on the loading dock, making sure every cubic inch of space was filled with ice. Making sure every truck had a solid day's work of deliveries. She had this nasty attitude and didn't care if she made employees uncomfortable." As Ferro finished speaking, his lips pressed tightly together.

"Was she like this in business only?"

"No. She was difficult virtually everywhere—and with virtually everyone."

"What do you mean?"

"My mother was a difficult person. And you didn't have to know her for her to be terrible to you."

I nodded and moved my hand forward, gesturing him to continue.

"She'd do things to strangers. For no reason. Like, stop in the entrance of a busy store to redo her lipstick. Or tie her shoe. She didn't care she was causing a commotion or if people were inconvenienced."

My eyes narrowed. "Intentionally be a thorn in someone's side?"

"Exactly."

I sat back and began sorting the information. With more inquiry, I'd come to know if this was true or if his perceptions were off the mark. Consistency in a person's narrative helps a therapist formulate what's real in a patient's life.

"If she knew the person behind her on the checkout line was in a rush, she'd deliberately sabotage things," he said.

"Like how?"

"Pay for something and then decide to have it voided. Use coins instead of dollars. Shit like that."

"How'd you know she was doing these things deliberately?"

"She'd tell us."

"Really?"

Ferro raised his voice a register. "Did you see how mad that guy was when I made the cashier ring up the groceries in three separate payments?"

My eyes widened taking this in.

"*Make me mad, you'll pay in spades* she'd always say."

"Sounds like your mother's a hostile person."

"Oh yeah. And no one was off limits."

"What does that mean?" I asked.

"She was an equal opportunity bitch. From dumping on employees to trashing her high-society friends. And everyone in between. She'd didn't care who you were."

"You said she did this *for no reason*. You don't really think that, do you?"

"I guess not. She must've had a reason. Her brand of crazy was everywhere."

"How was she with you?"

"Me?" His laugh was short and mirthless. "She made life unpleasant. Ever since I can remember."

"Tell me how she did this."

"Mostly with how she talked—and with looks," he said, suddenly struggling for words.

"What way did she talk to you?"

"She'd bitch and moan about everything I did. Her recent rants were about how her grandfather started this business and how it was a slap in the face to her—and all the Kingstons—that I had no interest in it."

I noticed Ferro was beginning to get emotional, and, little by little, his tone grew more forceful.

"She'd never let an opportunity slip by without telling me how journalism was nothing but junk food news."

"So, your mother didn't like your choice of career?"

"Not one bit," he said. "There was no way to please her."

I sat quietly taking this in and began to piece together his early history.

Sessions begin like a blank canvas. He was bringing color, texture, and tone to it.

"You said last session you never really spoke about what bothered you. You just worked on reducing the panic with techniques with your other therapist. And yet, as I hear you talking about your mother, you seem bothered, agitated."

"That's for shit sure."

Stillness, if used skillfully on a therapist's part, can allow a patient's thoughts and feelings to build and evolve. I fell quiet and waited to see where he would go within himself—and where he would take me as the session continued.

"As a little kid, she used to call me Luc-ass. Like, Luke's an ass."

"Terrible."

"The thing is, that was my mother all the way. If she didn't like you, you knew it."

"What about your brothers. Was she cruel to them?

"Wilson and Jackson, no." Lucas flicked a stray thread from his pants. "They were her pride and joy."

"Why do you say that?"

"They were identical twins. A built-in conversation piece for her. Like a magnet for attention. She lived for that. The attention and all."

"Do you feel any animosity toward your brothers?"

"They've always been good to me. Protective of me."

I leaned forward inviting him to speak more.

"I remember one time, when I was a kid, I wet the bed. My mother said she wouldn't have the maids change my sheets. But my brother, Jack, helped me take them off and wash them. He told me mom was just being mean and to ignore her. But when Wil found out, he went ballistic. He was all in her face, telling her she was a lousy mother. She just laughed at him and walked away."

"How old were you when this happened?"

"Like six or something. My brothers, thirteen."

I registered the pain he must have felt and shook my head in disapproval.

"When we were all together, she'd look at us and say our names. Jackson, Wil-son and Luc-ass. She always found it funny, but it wasn't. None of us ever laughed."

"Sounds like you got the short end of the stick."

"I fucking hated her for it." The sudden burst of emotion caused him discomfort. Lucas clenched his fists and huffed in lungful of air. "Aw, shit. I'm sorry."

"For what? Being angry and showing it?"

"I'm not good at it."

"I think you are. You expressed it pretty well right now. Maybe you feel discomfort afterwards for showing your real feelings?"

Ferro was quiet, nodding to himself, seemingly taking in what I had just said.

"It was always easier never to ask her for things. I avoided a lot of drama learning to get by on my own."

"So you learned very early her needs were not to be disrupted. Your needs had no worth."

"Something like that."

"That's tough to live with, Lucas."

The origin of his panic attacks could be rooted in his relationship with his mother. Not being able to be authentic, not having his needs met, and holding in negative feelings for the sake of self-preservation was a heavy burden for a little boy. And it would translate into a variety of unhealthy psychological forms as an adolescent and an adult.

"Where was your dad when all of this was going on?" I asked.

"If my mother was in the factory, he'd be in the office. If my mother was in the office, he'd be in the factory. If she was home, he tried his best not to be. He avoided her. He'd fly his plane to Atlantic City for the day or tinker with the muscle cars he bought over the years. He'd go and smoke a cigar in the orchard or say he ate a big lunch and wasn't hungry for dinner. Stuff like that."

"His staying away from her resulted in staying away from you too?" I asked.

Ferro narrowed his eyes, measuring my words. "I guess so."

So much multitasking goes on in analysis. I was listening to Ferro, indexing my own thoughts, wording my inquiries, and registering his conflicts. It occurred to me that addressing his father's abandonment was too premature. I wanted to pace the entry of unconscious material so it wouldn't overwhelm him. I returned to his mother.

"You mentioned your mom gave you looks," I said.

"She'd make this face like she thought I was so far beneath her."

Again, my diagnostic skills were busy working, but I showed him nothing beyond interest in what he was saying.

"You know, she slipped on some ice in the docking area, hit the ground, and died. The autopsy said death was instantaneous."

"Broken neck?"

"No. Brain hemorrhage." Slowly, Ferro leaned forward and engaged me with his eyes. "Okay. Time to be honest." Like telling a secret, he said in a hushed tone, "I hoped she suffered when she died."

I was quiet for a moment and offered my thoughts. "That makes sense to me."

"It does?"

I nodded. "Why do you think it makes sense to me, Lucas?"

Ferro was quiet again. But it was a quietness full of activity. "I wanted her to suffer—because she made *me* suffer," he said.

Knowing how rejection, hurt, and abandonment creates anger and rage, I didn't hesitate. I nodded in agreement. "She hurt you too deeply and too often," I said. "And when she wasn't hurting you, you saw her hurting others."

Ferro moved his shoulders forward and closed his eyes.

"Maybe you have these paralyzing attacks because you don't give yourself permission to feel this kind of anger."

Lucas said nothing. He stared at his sneakers, suddenly subdued.

"What you've mentioned so far suggests there wasn't a lot of room to be real with your feelings, especially the negative ones like disappointment, anger, frustration."

Lucas nodded.

"It didn't occur to me till now, but what do your friends call you?"

"Luke. They call me Luke," he said. "I hate Lucas."

"Why didn't you correct me when I kept calling you Lucas?" I delved deeper. "Do you feel I'd give you a look or embarrass you?"

"No, I don't think you'd ever do that."

"I'll call you Luke, then."

He looked at me for a moment, narrowing his eyes. "I'd like that."

We lapsed into a long silence. Often silence has its own texture, and this one felt like a shared space where one moment was going to link to another in a powerful way.

"Are you married?" Luke asked, noticing the gold ring on my left hand.

His question took me by surprise and made my stomach pitch. In therapy, patients often ask therapists personal questions. Sometimes these questions can distract from the patient's treatment. While other times, personal questions can enhance the therapy. I decided to answer Luke because I sensed he needed to know more about me in order to trust me.

"Yes, I am—*was* married."

"Are you divorced? Separated?"

I drew in a slow breath and felt the numbness begin to take form. "My husband died not too long ago."

"That sucks."

"Cancer," I said, hoping my disclosure would ease the awkwardness that filled the room.

"Got kids?"

"By the time we were ready, he needed chemo, and, well, it just wasn't in the cards."

"Maybe that's a good thing. It'd be hard for kids to go through that."

"Mmmm. Would've been difficult."

Luke sat back in his chair, seemingly stirred by my brief, yet personal offerings. His posture softened, and his eyes widened. "I guess you could say death is something we have in common."

"Has it been hard for you? Moving through *your* mother's death?" I asked.

"Nope. My mother dying was a relief."

Death can summon a myriad of emotions in a person. Loss of a loved one can flood an individual's psyche with pain, anguish, and despair. For another, death can be a freeing experience, liberating a once-tortured soul. Losing Ryan collapsed my world, but Luke's mother's death brought relief to his. In my line of work, I never judged how a patient experienced death. I only sought to understand and to learn.

"There's your honesty again," I said.

"Well, you said it'd be important."

"It is. And will continue to be important, Luke."

And with that, the session ended.

Notes

Excellent second session. Signed releases and completed medical, mental health and family history.

At present, reports sleep disturbances, poor appetite. Chronic neck and back pain. Last physical December 2016, no allergies, surgeries, or hospitalizations. Ulcer in college.

Denies any current substance use, but drinks on occasion. Not taking any medication for anxiety. Denies any suicidal or homicidal thoughts or intentions. No previous mental health treatment with other therapists before working with Dr. Karne. Reports not being honest before in treatment. Prefers being called Luke.

<u>Transference:</u> Still positive.

<u>Counter-transference:</u> Positive. Though I wondered if patient followed me home, he didn't seem too offended when I asked if it was him. Find Luke likeable though. Insightful with a sense of humor. Find myself feeling invigorated by session.

<u>Relevant issues:</u> Mother's death January this year. Moved back from Florida to New York. Living alone for first time in his life, Condo in Dix Hills. Also new job—all significant stressors.

Luke details early life with his mother as cold, critical, neglectful, and emotionally abusive. Will further explore mother-son bond.

Father absent, aloof. Need to find out more here too. Good connection to older twin brothers. However, attachment injuries from parents leave Luke angry, disappointed.

Could early childhood trauma be related to panic? Is this Luke's way of getting the nurturance he needed? Or does panic rise because he has trouble with anger and rage? What other unfulfilled needs are there?

<u>Diagnosis:</u> Panic disorder, but will look to rule out borderline personality, depression. Will continue to assess.

<u>Prognosis:</u> Good.

Wednesday Night

I was surprised nearly an hour passed since writing my clinical notes, but dwelling in such analytic moments often suspended me in time. I went through the motions to lock up, but as I shut the blinds, I saw it again. A long dark sedan in the parking lot.

"What the hell..."

It crept slowly across the empty spaces and disappeared around the bend. Without hesitating, I ran out of the office, slamming the door shut. I hurled myself down the each of the stairwells to the proceeding landing and emerged from the lobby exit like a bat out of hell. There was only one way in and out of the office complex, and I knew I'd get there before the car did.

I barreled onto the pavement as the headlights emerged from the building's corner. The beams curled in the humid air and slowly inched upward revealing my presence. It took a second, but I saw it wasn't the dark sedan I'd seen, but rather Steve in the security truck.

"Dammit." I dropped my briefcase and bag in defeat.

"Out for a late night jog, Doc?" Steve asked as he rolled up.

"Did you see a long black sedan?"

"You expecting someone?"

"I saw this car—from the window."

Steve looked over his shoulder toward the far end of the parking lot, shining his flashlight in one sweeping stroke. Then he walked a few steps in the other direction.

"For the last hour, it's been just your car and my truck here in the lot. Before that, a red Porsche."

"My last patient," I said, nodding.

"You okay?" Steve sensed my fear and put his arm around me.

I brushed away his concern and stepped back. "You might not have seen it if you were making your rounds."

"Seen what? Another car?" Steve clipped his flashlight to his belt.

"Yes," I said hiking my hands on my hips.

"Listen, I've been in the kiosk for the last hour. And I would've passed any vehicles in the lot as I made my rounds. No way a car came in and left without me knowing."

I considered his words as I looked around the parking lot again. Before I turned back to Steve, my eyes lingered on the security truck.

Dark gray can look black from far away, I thought. *And Steve drives the perimeter at a turtle's pace.*

"Someone bothering you, Doc? Any trouble I gotta know about?"

"Just seeing things, I guess."

"Lemme walk you to your car."

"No, I'm good now."

"Sorry. Not taking no for an answer," he said, pressing his thick hand against my back.

I picked up my bag and briefcase and slung them over my shoulders. I fiddled for my car keys and chirped the alarm off.

"You ain't watching any of those slasher movies now, are you?" Steve raised his eyebrows. "Saw...Son of Saw...The Saw That Ate Manhattan. My grandkids can't get enough of them."

"Nah. I stay away from the blood and guts ones."

"I'm partial to the Buddy Movie genre, myself. Martin and Lewis. Hope and Crosby."

"Hepburn and Tracy," I added.

"Matthau and Lemmon. Don't make 'em like that anymore."

"They sure don't."

Steve opened the door and waited for me to climb into the driver's seat.

"Thanks, Steve. I don't know what I'd do without you."

"No thanks needed. It's what I'm here for."

Steve waved me off as I left the parking lot. I had the intention of heading home, but seeing Steve in the truck didn't satisfy me. My mind leapt to Luke. And this was the second time my thoughts linked Luke with feelings of dread.

I doubt Luke could've driven home, changed cars, and been back to my office in under an hour. My reasoning didn't settle the eeriness I felt. I knew what I had to do—and I caught my reflection in the rear view mirror. It seemed to scowl back at me as I recalled Luke's address.

"Just driving by isn't a bad thing," I said to my reflection. "I'll put an end to these worries once and for all."

It didn't take long to get to the Long Island Expressway and head east to Bagatelle Road to Dix Hills, where Luke lived. Though it took a few turnarounds, I found my way to the Townhouse Colony Estates. My heartbeat was rapid, and my breathing was heavy as I entered the development.

Moving down the softly-lit street, I tried to recall Luke's house number. *Was it twenty-two? Or two twenty-three?* I thought as I rolled into the maze of townhouses.

Feeling open to the elements, I clicked the car lights off and dimmed the Saab's dashboard. I never crossed any boundaries with a patient and worried its glow would expose me and my sudden lapse of my reasoning. As I edged past number twenty-three, I saw a silver mustang in the driveway. *No Porsche.*

In the minutes that passed on the way to the two hundred's section, I felt more self-consciousness. I reached into the back of the passenger seat and grabbed Ryan's Mets cap. I threw it on and tucked my long hair under its rim. I snaked around each of the curves in the road and peered at each house's number.

"Two hundred fifteen. Two hundred seventeen. Two hundred nineteen," I counted aloud, hoping my own voice would ground me somehow. As I passed two hundred twenty one, I saw it. A red Porsche was in the driveway of two hundred twenty three. I cruised slowly, noticing that, through the windows, the lights were on. I saw a flickering television too. In the darkness, it was hard to see more, but I felt relieved.

"Just my imagination," I muttered as I made the drive home.

Session Three

Friday, June 9th

L uke was pale when I opened the door.

"You okay?"

He remained in his seat in the waiting room, seemingly unable to move. "I'm...I'm feeling anxious right now."

"Right this second?"

"Yeah."

I moved into the waiting room, but he held his hand up toward me.

"Just...just gimme a minute."

I watched as Luke closed his eyes tightly. He remained still but slowed his breathing. It was quite a while before he stood up and walked into the consultation room. As he passed, I saw a worn, brown satchel slung over his shoulder, the kind college students use to carry books.

I closed the door and walked to my desk. Luke sat down slowly, shifting his body in small tight movements. He seemed so fragile—like at any moment he could break into pieces. He hesitated where to put the satchel.

First, he set it on the floor, then the other side of his chair. Finally, he picked it up and put it in his lap, leaning it slightly against his chest.

"You've been practicing the breathing skills I taught you."

"I'm getting better at it." Luke swept his hair away from his eyes and cleared his throat. Then he looked directly at me. "I'm ready to talk about what's bothering me."

"Hold on a second now. If you're feeling this panicked, maybe you're not really ready."

"No, I am."

"Well, okay then."

"I'd like to show you something." Luke unzipped the satchel and pulled out a thick folder. "It's a piece I wrote for *The Miami Press*."

Luke leafed through the portfolio of his professional work and handed a clipping to me.

"Concern Grows for Missing Broward County Man," I read aloud. "Luke Ferro, Staff Writer."

"I don't like to show this piece."

"Why's that?" I glanced at the article again. It was a short feature on page two, a prominent placement in any newspaper, and a jewel in the crown for any young writer. I read it in full to myself:

> Miami, Florida: The search for a twenty-two year old man resumed Monday after heavy rains delayed the investigation. Police and several dozen volunteers continued looking for any signs of Donald Gallin, who was last seen at Club Camber, a trendy nightspot in South Beach, one week ago. "Authorities have many clues but no leads, yet feel strongly foul play is involved," said Karen Marie Eeds, a family friend involved in the search. Police confirm Gallin's blood-smeared car was found in a wooded area, two miles from Club Camber. "An obvious struggle took place in the vehicle and we know robbery was not a motive," Dade County Sheriff John Perembrooke said. A $50,000 reward has been posted for any information that can help authorities in the case.

"I. . . I know..." Luke's voice trailed off to a whisper.

I lifted my eyes back to him. "I couldn't hear you Luke. What did you say?"

"I said, I know where he is."

Confused, I looked hard at the article again. My eyes caught the words *nightclub—struggle—blood.* "You know where he is?"

Luke's eyes locked into mine. "Yeah."

"How can you possibly know where he is?"

Luke clutched the arms of the chair and jutted his chin out. "Because I killed him."

I heard the words, but they were muffled in my ears. I understood the words but couldn't make the leap in my mind. I tried to ground myself, but I was going somewhere else. *No leads—Foul play—Grieving family.*

When the real and the unreal collide, a moment of denial crashes within a person's psyche. Though it was only seconds, the shock of it all moved me in slow motion. I put down the paper and focused on Luke. I saw him struggling to breathe. Fighting the pressuring panic, he suddenly doubled over onto the floor. The folder he held fell along with him, scattering the clippings everywhere.

I wasn't prepared for anything like this. I thought the panic disorder could be traced to his dysfunctional mother, but this changed everything. A sudden expanse swelled within me, and it took all I had to push aside my fear. I managed to move out of my chair toward Luke and knelt on the floor.

"Luke," I called out, struggling to roll him onto his back.

His body was limp, and his face was cold to the touch. I checked his pulse and shook him again.

"Luke, can you hear me?"

Suddenly his eyes flew open. As his pupils dilated, I sat back on my heels.

"Stay there. Don't move."

I picked up the stream of pages and placed them back into his folder, clearing a path for me to walk.

"Deep breath in, purse it out."

Luke did this without hesitation.

And so did I.

I ran into the bathroom and soaked some paper towels with cold water, wondering as I studied my face in the mirror if Prader was right. Maybe this case would be too much for me.

I've heard many sad stories from the patients who allow me into their lives—stories of disgrace, regret, accounts of ruin and humiliation. Stories of pain and trauma. Narratives of personal collapse and loss.

And death.

Death, which happens suddenly, from a catastrophe or accident. Or gradually, from illness or disease. But death had never been revealed in this way to me.

I thought about this young man. I thought about his family. And then I thought about Luke.

I brought back the damp towels and placed them across his forehead. Luke didn't react. He was like a lifeless marionette, strings cut. I found a nearby blanket and draped it over him, and then pulled up a chair next to him.

"You okay?" I asked as he opened his eyes.

He didn't move but whispered, "Yes."

"You let it out," I said in a voice expressing both astonishment and reassurance.

"I d-id," he said in broken syllables. "You won't t-ell anyone."

"I won't."

Every psychologist has a duty to warn and protect people from patients who pose a serious threat of violence, but that duty applies to foreseeable harm. What's in the past is not reportable.

A different kind of silence fell into the room.

It felt heavy.

It was profound.

And we remained in it for the rest of the session.

Notes

Luke says he killed a man. Knows where he is. Passes out after disclosure. There was a "struggle." There was "blood." Need more details. Do I access the internet—or old school newspaper search in the library?

Event is in the past so no Duty to Warn ethics apply. Is this death an accident? A murder? Absolutely terrifying session.

Transference: Luke is still connected to me in a positive way. Trusts me enough to share this secret. I'm worried if he can stay positive when I ask for more details.

Counter-transference: Incredible terror and fear. Confusion about his story. Connected to patient but now I feel very, very guarded.

Am I in danger knowing this?

Can I trust him?

There was a reason I felt all those unsettling, eerie feelings days ago. My perceptions weren't off or exaggerated. Luke was holding a terrible secret. That's what this is. This is a form of projective introjection.

Relevant issues: Left message with Dr. Prader for immediate supervision on this case. Urgent I see her ASAP. Scheduled session for tomorrow.

Diagnosis: Presenting diagnosis is Panic disorder, but need to rule out psychopathy, borderline personality, intermittent explosive disorder.

Prognosis: Uncertain.

Friday Night

In this day and age of internet tracking, a search for Donald Gallin's death might be detected. I stopped the urge to do a Google search, logged off the computer, and clicked the laptop shut. It was also vital to protect the confidentiality of Luke's disclosure despite the unfolding darkness.

I walked to the picture window and watched the wind blow the rectangular shaped sailcloth that shaded the lanai in the restaurant next door. It tugged at its trusses in short, taut jerks. A storm was coming, and the strengthening wind threw strands of black and gray across the sky.

As the rain began to fall, I reminded myself that without the promise of complete confidentiality, psychotherapy can't work. Doctor-patient privilege protects from intrusions of others—from family members to legal and governmental meddling. Therapists fiercely guard safeguarding personal disclosures so therapeutic work can be done—even if things shared by patients are unforgivable acts of cruelty or evil.

At times, though, a therapist *has* to breach the privilege—if a patient is going to hurt himself or another person. It's called a *Duty to Warn.*

I sat on the ledge of the window and let my mind wander to the story responsible for law.

In 1976, a University of California student, Prosenjit Poddar, was in therapy with a psychologist from the university's health center. His treatment focused on a recent rejection he had from a young woman named Tatiana Tarasoff. During one of the sessions, the psychologist learned of Poddar's murderous intention to kill Tarasoff and reported to the police his plans. The police questioned Mr. Poddar and found him rational and reasonable—and not an immediate threat. The police made Poddar promise to stay away from Tarasoff. Neither the therapist nor the police department contacted Tatiana Tarasoff though—and two months later, Poddar shot and killed her.

Deborah Serani

This murder raised the issue that privilege and confidentiality end when public peril begins. When a patient identifies a third party as being in harm's way, a therapist must do everything to contact authorities.

But because Donald Gallin was dead, I could do nothing It was in the past. Not pressing—and I wasn't allowed to break privilege or breach confidentiality. Thinking about these things helped me calm down. I stretched my shoulders and rolled my neck from side to side, feeling the tightness loosen.

Then I walked back to my desk and took out the article, this time studying the small, set-in picture of Donald Gallin.

It was a portrait shot, graduation from high school or possibly college. The picture was grainy, but it was easy to see a glow of happiness in his eyes.

"Goddammit," I said.

I shut the file and stuffed it into my briefcase. I tended to the office, closing things down for the weekend. Sorting patient files, locking the file cabinet, clearing the desk.

Then the plants and trees got their weekly watering. I listened as the soil soaked up the water. Then I removed the dying growths to help the new sprouts thrive. Finally, I closed all the windows and angled the blinds so they could get all the light they needed till I returned on Monday.

Then I called Dr. Prader.

Supervision

Saturday, June 10

❝Thanks for squeezing me in this morning."

"Your message said it was urgent."

"It's the patient I spoke about earlier this week."

"The one you thought showed up at your house?" she asked. "You were right?"

"No. It wasn't him."

"You confronted him?"

"Well, yes. I did. But to be sure, I drove by his house."

Prader said nothing, but disapproval was obvious in her hard-boiled stare.

"We can talk about the meaning behind my drive-by later. There's something more important, though."

Prader took out her file and waited.

"I don't even know where to begin."

I took a long breath. I wasn't able to speak the words and readied myself to sign.

"Don't, Alicia. If it's something this big, you need to speak it aloud."

She's right, I said to myself—and agreed not to sign anymore in the session. "I think he killed a young man," I finally said.

"First you think he followed you home, and *now* you think he killed a man?"

"I don't *think* he killed a man. I know it."

Prader said nothing but shifted back in her chair.

"Luke handed me a news article he wrote about a missing man during the session. Then he had a fierce panic attack and passed out on the floor."

"What was in the article?"

I reached into my handbag and retrieved a copy of the article. I grabbed a marker on the desk and carefully blotted out Luke's name and other identifying information. Prader slid her glasses low on her nose, read it, and remained silent for a moment.

"He said he knows where he is," I continued. "I don't know all the details though."

Prader pursed her lips.

"I realize why I've had all those eerie feelings since meeting him."

"Yes, this man may be dangerous," Prader finally said.

"I know."

"You need to make some decisions here. First, you need to carefully consider *if* you should work with this patient—and then you need to ask yourself *why* you would *want* to work with this patient."

She took in a deep breath and leaned closer toward me.

"Second, if you make the decision to go forward and discover details about this young man, you know none of this can be reported to anyone," Prader said.

"I know—"

"Wait, I'm not finished. You'll need to set a firm treatment frame with clear boundaries of how the work will proceed."

"I'm prepared to do all that."

"Okay. Now *why* do you want to work with this patient?"

"A case like this could help me move out of the numbness I sometimes feel."

"It could," Prader said. "We choose to work with patients for many reasons."

"A difficult case would pull me into the present and away from the past."

"And if it's too much to manage, you'll refer it out?"

"Of course," I said.

Prader lowered her eyes and studied the article again. I watched as she tracked each word. "A long time ago, when I was a grad student, I worked at Rikers Island doing therapy. All of the prisoners were difficult cases. Some more than others. But I enjoyed the work. It was exciting dealing with pathology that intense."

"So, you get it?" I asked.

Prader nodded. "But, the guards were right outside the offices in the counseling center. If an inmate raised his voice or became physically agitated, within seconds, the door opened." Prader leaned closer to me. "You don't have security in your office, keeping you safe if something escalated. It's only you. And the patient."

"True," I said.

"I understand the pull a case like has, Alicia. He's probably verbal and insightful—but you have to think about safety."

Safety was something most Coda's knew in life. When I was young, I'd always take care that Nicole's needs and feelings were understood by the neighborhood hearing kids. I learned fast to protect her and my parents from the hurtful things many hearing people said by leaving out the cruel remarks as I interpreted.

Then there were times I'd make sure the house was safe—that windows and doors were locked, that the stove and oven were off. My parents and sister wouldn't be able to hear if a burglar entered or if a fire broke out.

"I have my panic alarm. And I'll ask the security guard on the grounds to keep an eye on my office."

"Sounds like you *have* given this some thought."

"I have."

"When the internship at Riker's was offered, I was the first to apply in my class," Prader said. "At the time, I was interested in Rehabilitation Psychology. The work was immensely profound, but it was more frightening than rewarding."

"How so?"

"The pathology the inmates had. It was so static- -so unfixable. For the most part, treatment was a failure there. It was hard to accept that."

I nodded and listened attentively. It was always special to learn something about Dr. Prader. She rarely shared personal stories because supervision focused on me and my needs.

"So, I made my way here," she continued. "Hospital work as a shrink is more rewarding. And patients go home feeling better than when they arrived."

"So, you've worked with patients with serious pathology."

"Yes. And while the work can be fascinating, I'm on the fence with this one, Alicia."

"I understand. I'm guarded too."

"Well, maybe you're right. Working a difficult case could be a good thing for you," she said, jotting down notes. "Don't hesitate to call before we meet again on Tuesday. Especially if something doesn't feel right."

"I will."

Saturday Night

"This is operator 4297 at New York Relay. What number do you want to call?"

"I'd like to call 555-2080," I said, getting into the car.

"I'll be off the line until the TTY user connects," she said, placing me on hold.

After a few seconds, I was reconnected. "This is Nicole, go ahead," the relay operator said, reading Nicole's text telephone words.

"It's Alicia. Are we still on for dinner? Should I pick up a cheesecake from Mae's? Go ahead."

"Totally. The kids are excited, and Keith's getting the BBQ all ready," the relay operator said.

I heard the soft breathing of the operator as she clicked away on the TTY keys. Conversations like these were never private, but I couldn't Facetime with Nicole while driving. So, relay services were the next best thing.

"Where you been anyway? I've been trying to track you down," the relay operator continued.

"Been dealing with a difficult case. Stressed about it, so I went to supervision. Go ahead," I said back.

"Well, the kids baked a cake, so come straight here. SK," said the operator, letting me know Nicole had *stopped keying*, done with the conversation.

"Okay. SK, SK," I said to the operator, giving the code for I've *stopped keying* too.

"Your party has signed off, Ma'am," the operator said.

"Thank you," I replied, turning off the Bluetooth.

I drove to Nicole's as a light cascade of rain fell on the hot asphalt of the parkway. I noticed the steam rose in strands of sheer mist and then evaporated into nothingness.

To offset the dreary atmosphere, I popped in a Beatles CD and cranked up the volume. Before long, I was singing with Paul, George, and John and drumming along with Ringo on the steering wheel.

The sun broke through the clouds as I headed south on Manetto Hill Road, and once I crossed the parkway bridge, it stopped completely. I suddenly found myself hoping everyone would be up for a swim in the pool after dinner. I needed to be in the water, floating lightly.

As I turned into Quentin Court, the comforting thoughts ended. My adrenaline surged when I saw two Nassau County Police cars near Nicole's house. I screeched the Saab to a halt, bolted out of the car, and approached the officer sitting in his vehicle.

"What's going on?"

"Are you Mrs. Rahm? Soraya Rahm?"

"Uh, no," I said holding my hand to my chest. My eyes moved from Nicole's house to the adjacent neighbor. "I'm visiting my sister, next door."

"There's been a burglary, Ma'am," he said.

I chewed my bottom lip as I looked around the area. The entire cul-de-sac was quiet, no signs of life anywhere.

Perfect conditions for a crime, I thought.

Just as I brought my focus back to the officer, I saw Nicole turn the corner with Shasta on her leash.

"*That's* my sister," I said, raising my hand in the air. "She might know where Soraya is."

The officer peered at Nicole through his department issued aviators.

I took in a deep breath, relieved to see her in the distance. "Officer, what's your name?"

"Waldman."

"Alicia Reese." I shook his hand. "My sister's Deaf, but she lip reads. She's pretty awesome. But if you'd like me to interpret, just say so."

"Won't be necessary," Waldman said, unconcerned.

He took off his sunglasses and inserted them carefully in his chest pocket. Then he softened his posture by placing his hands behind his back, feet apart—like a soldier's fall-out and rest. But something about his demeanor suggested he had experiences with Deaf people before. I always trusted that instinct whenever I felt it.

Shasta didn't sense the same because she barked as she trotted closer to

Waldman. Immediately, Nicole pulled on the orange lead to hold her back.

"It's okay, girl," she said as they both slowed to a walk.

I stepped off the curb to meet them.

"What? What?" Nic signed, agitated.

I held out my right two fingers, stuck them under my left arm, and pulled them away. "Burglary."

"Shit," she said aloud. "Just now?"

"I guess so," I said. Then I pointed to the officer and signed. "This is Detective Waldman."

Waldman looked into Nicole's eyes and shook her hand. He kept his gaze directly on her and spoke so she could see his lips – the way a person familiar with Deaf culture would know how to do.

"Do you have any idea where Mrs. Rahm might be? We got a call from the central station alarm at four o'clock this afternoon, but we can't reach her at her contact numbers," he said.

"She's away for the weekend. A cousin's wedding in Massachusetts," Nicole signed as I translated. "I'm taking her paper and mail while she's gone."

"You have any contact numbers besides her cell?"

"No, but her brother's nearby. Lives in Hicksville. Rajesh Tansoo."

Waldman jotted the name down.

"Officer, what happened?" Nicole asked aloud.

"A cursory check of the house showed a break-in," he said, keeping eye contact with Nicole. "Closets and drawers were tossed in one room. We call it a grab-and-go."

Nicole blinked in disbelief, as did I.

"According to the alarm company, the motion detector tripped the siren. Suspects couldn't have gotten away with too much." Waldman unsnapped his radio from his belt loop and turned to the side. "Scott, I got neighbors."

"Copy. I'm Side C," a voice said.

"Affirmative." Waldman looked back at Nicole and me. "Detective Scott is in the back. He'll take it from here. Just don't touch anything till the crime lab arrives."

After thanking Waldman, Nicole, Shasta, and I walked up the driveway. As we continued along to the backyard, we found Detective Scott taking notes by a broken window. The screen was on the ground, stripped of its metal wiring, and the glass was fully opened to its sash. There were scuffmarks on the vinyl siding underneath and around the frame, as well as footprints, which flattened the thick grass. Taking all this in, we made sure not to let Shasta venture closer.

Scott stuck his pen behind his ear and flicked the notepad closed. He busied himself with getting the pad into his suit pocket, not looking up as Nicole spoke.

"I'm Soraya's neighbor, Nicole Cappas."

"What about a cactus?" Scott asked.

Nicole looked away for a moment, irritated. She was used to hearing people not knowing how important it was to look at Deaf people when they talked. Doing so made it easy to read lips. Not just for the Deaf person, but also the hearing person. If Detective Scott focused on his conversation with Nicole, he wouldn't have misunderstood her. "Cappas" wouldn't be "cactus."

Scott saw the "Hearing Dog" emblem on Shasta's orange leash and vest and shifted his attitude.

"I'm Nicole Cappas," she said again, articulating and overstating her words. "I live next door."

"Yes, of course. Mrs. Cappas." He extended his hand. "I'm Detective Randy Scott."

Nicole turned and signed to Shasta that it was time to sit and rest.

"I'm Alicia Reese, her sister," I signed and said aloud, introducing myself to Scott.

"It'd be a lot easier if you translated for me," Scott said, his eyes glued to the windowpane instead of us. "I don't have time to babysit you guys."

"He wants me to translate, okay?" I signed, raising my eyebrows to Nicole who was already rolling hers back to me in imitation. Then I slipped my hand to my side and signed "Asshole," to her—out of eyesight of Scott.

Nicole smirked.

"So what happened here?" I said to Scott.

"Looks like each entry was checked to see if it was unlocked. Suspects created their own access here. It's the most remote part of the house." Scott pointed around the area as he talked. "Cut the screen, smashed the window, climbed in. Worked the room, took whatever they could—fled through the front door when the motion detector went off."

I listened to Scott and then signed to Nicole.

"So, you think more than one person?" I asked after reading Nicole's signs.

"We're thinking that. One keepin' a look out while the other breaks in. Could also be one suspect running the whole show," Scott said, opening his notepad. "Crime scene should be able to tell us. They'll be here soon."

"Can't believe this happened. Shasta and I just left for a walk. Maybe ten or fifteen minutes ago," Nicole signed.

I translated back to Scott.

"These things can happen fast. Mrs. Rahm did all the right things, though. Alarm system. Signage on the property. Doors and windows locked." Scott slipped the pen from his ear back into his hand and jotted more notes. "Not much more anyone coulda done. Sometimes bad things just happen."

My hands fluttered at lightning speed as I signed what Scott said for Nicole.

"Good no one was home when this happened," I said.

Scott tightened his lips and nodded. "Burglary's *always* better than robbery. Mrs. Cappas, did you notice any vehicles while you were out?" Scott asked, finally looking at Nicole as he spoke.

"No cars," she signed.

"What about people?" he asked. "Anyone suspicious?"

"No. Nothing," she said aloud.

"Have there been other burglaries in the neighborhood, Detective?" I asked.

"No," Scott said. "Reports of Juvees taking batting practice with mailboxes though."

Sensing there wasn't much more to talk about, Scott asked for Nicole's name and contact information, which she jotted down, herself, in his notepad. As we headed back toward the front of the house, Officer Waldman was checking the contents of the Rahm mailbox.

"Some mail here for you, Mrs. Cappas," he said, waiting until she was in lip-reading distance to speak.

"That happens." Nicole smiled. "Postal workers mix up our mail sometimes. Can I take it, or is this evidence?"

Waldman looked at Scott, who hiked his shoulders and waved off his consent. "No, you can have it," Waldman said and handed it to Nicole.

Just before we made our way back to Nicole's house, Waldman asked if he could pet Shasta.

"Sure," Nicole replied.

Not everyone who's Deaf needs or wants a Hearing Dog, but when I was growing up, Nicole really wanted one. Though she was an independent and fierce girl, with a history of kicking my ass and anyone else's in the neighborhood, Nicole loved animals and always wanted a dog of her own. Hearing Dogs can help Deaf people hear things many hearing people take for granted. The noise of an oncoming car. A police siren. An approaching ambulance. A whistling teakettle. A microwave ding. So just before graduating high school, Nicole began working with Cocoa, an Akita German Shepard mix. Cocoa went to college with her at Gallaudet University—and then to work when Nicole became a graphic artist in New York City. Ten years or so later, Shasta, a golden retriever, joined Nicole and Keith just before they got married.

Shasta was instrumental in helping Nicole adjust when the twins were born. It always amazed me seeing how she alerted Nicole when the babies were fussing. Or crying. Or when they awoke from a nap. Even now, as I watched Shasta's protectiveness of Nicole with the police officers, I felt a profound admiration for the bond they shared.

"Beautiful dog," Waldman signed. His signs were slow and hesitant as if he was trying to get the movements down just right.

"Wow," Nicole signed back.

I smiled, admiring this gesture of connection.

"How do you know sign?" I asked.

"My neighbor growing up was Deaf. She used to teach me signs," Waldman said and signed simultaneously.

"That's so cool," Nicole said.

"Yeah. Anyway, just let us know if hear from Mrs. Rahm—or if anything else comes to mind," Waldman said, handing Nicole his contact card.

"Sure thing," Nicole said.

Then she turned toward Shasta and signaled him. Nicole took her right hand and pinched her fingers together. She moved them to her mouth, almost touching her lips and then to the side of her right cheek.

"Home," she signed.

Session Four

Monday, June 12th

❝Luke, I'd like to do a session on the couch today."

"Why?"

"By lying on the couch, two things happen. First, it helps reduce anxiety."

"So maybe there won't be another panic attack?"

"Yes.

"Second, it makes it easier for you to concentrate on inner experiences without being distracted by me. Resting on the couch gives us a better way to manage things before they get too big."

"So, just lie down here?"

"Yes. I'll be sitting off to the side of you, out of your line of vision. But if you feel uncomfortable, just sit up, okay?"

Luke nodded walked over to the couch. Using his hands as leverage, he placed his body slowly across its line of cushions. He moved the pillow a few times to get comfortable. Then he crossed his feet and rested his intertwined fingers across his broad chest.

"Tell me how you're feeling now?"

"It's weird not seeing you."

"I know. It may take some getting used to, but let's give it a try."

Allowing a therapist into the margins of pain and dread, of shame and humiliation takes great courage on the part of the patient. I never minimized how hard it was to take that step. I waited for him to start the session.

"You must think I'm a monster or something."

"Our work is to help make sense of what happened, not sit in judgment of it."

Luke was quiet. Sensing he was adrift in his thoughts, I gave him a starting point.

"What happened that night?"

"My friends and me—we went to a new club. A place that had shadow dancers. Y'know, when girls dance behind a screen?"

"Mhmm."

"I was standing at the bar getting a beer when one of the dancers sat down next to me. She had this long hair, below her waist. I don't throw lines around, but she was a great dancer. And I wanted to tell her. I started to talk to her, but she threw her hand up in my face—like she didn't want to be bothered with me."

"She rejected you."

"Yeah. And I thought to myself, *If you don't want to talk, don't come out to the bar.*"

"Did you say that to her?"

"No. Said nothing. Got my beer and went back to my friends."

"Did they see what happened?"

"The place was really crowded. So, no, they couldn't see the bar."

Luke was quiet for a long while. It was important for him to talk uninterrupted. When he spoke again, his speech was slow and labored. There were many pauses, and, at times, his voice was slight, like wisps of air.

"But there was this guy who *did* see what happened. At the bar. He laughed at me."

"Was this guy Donald Gallin?"

Luke nodded. "I drank my beer. Had a few more and left on my own because my friends wanted to stay longer. When I got to the parking lot, I saw him out there. He was walking to his car too. I can't remember, but the next thing I knew I hauled my fist into his face."

I said nothing as I sat further back in my chair and took in a deep, quiet breath.

"His car door was open, so I dragged him in—cracked his head against the steering wheel. Did it another time, busting his front teeth out. Damn, the blood went everywhere."

I listened, motionless. But I felt the blow of his every word in my own gut.

"He didn't fight back. Didn't even yell out. I pushed him into the passenger seat and got in the car. Found the keys and drove off."

I fought the mounting anxiety and struggled to keep my focus. I needed to search for the psychological conflicts, the origins of pathology, and anything clinical I could grasp.

"Drove for a while, in circles mostly. But then I stopped and pulled the car off the road, into the woods. Next thing I know, I'm standing over him. He was groaning, trying to speak."

Luke was quiet for another long moment.

"As I hear myself—it's horrible what I did. I feel ashamed. But it's like it wasn't even me doing it."

"Let's put shame on the sidelines for now. It's important to tell your story. To free yourself from this terrible secret."

"He tried to get away, crawling on his hands and knees, but I kicked him down. Then I jammed my knee in his back and grabbed his neck."

I felt dizzy, and a disgust churned within me. I sensed those things in Luke as well. His voice became sharper and more amplified, as did his breathing.

"Next thing I remember—I snapped my hand all the way back. I felt the break of his neck run through his body."

I felt a chill creep along my skin as I cataloged feelings. Though I had so many questions, I remained still.

"When he was dead, I realized what I did. I freaked out. Up till then, there was like two of me. One that didn't care and another that was just watching."

"How'd you freak out?"

"I went apeshit. Couldn't believe what I did. Got so fucking sick I choked on my own puke and threw up."

"What happened next, Luke?"

"Somehow I got home. Must've gone back to the club to get my car, 'cause when I woke up the next morning, it was there at my apartment. Got rid of my clothes. My sneakers. Tossed them all in the garbage. Then took a long shower. My roommate, Jeff, came in around four a.m. He was totally shitfaced."

Luke rubbed his hands over his face and exhaled heavily.

"Next day I called in sick. All I did was look at the news and listen to the radio—y'know, to see if anyone found him. I was a fucking mess. I couldn't stop thinking of about it. What I'd done. Even thought about confessing."

"You did?"

"Thought of other things too. Calling anonymously. Leaving a note. But none of those were good. I mean, c'mon, no way I was gonna let myself go to jail for this."

As I watched him lying on the couch, I slipped my trembling hand in my pocket and found the panic alarm. I lifted it out and placed it on the desk so it was readily accessible.

"After a couple of days, I went back, to make sure no one could find him. I parked my car about a mile away, far into the woods. I took out a bucket I had in the trunk I used to hold tools and grabbed a shovel. Then I walked to his car, staying away from the road."

"You walked along the wood's line?"

"Yeah. Didn't want anyone to see me. When I got there, I saw the car was in the same place. The keys still in the ignition. Saw him on the ground. Just like I left him."

Luke was quiet for a moment. From where I was sitting, I saw him close his eyes.

"I don't know how long it took, but I made a big enough ditch to bury him. Then I turned the bucket over and sat down on it to catch my breath. But I couldn't catch it. Couldn't breathe. It was like the dirt was everywhere. In my nose. My mouth. My throat. I think I puked a few times."

Luke's eyes flew open.

"Took off my shirt. Used it to get the dirt off. It didn't help much though. But I was able to breathe again. Then I went back to his car, got in, and drove it near where my car was. Found a spot and parked it there. I wiped everything down. Everything."

"What happened next?"

"Walked back to my car, making sure to stay away from the road. Counted three cars that drove past. A red Honda Accord. Old yellow Subaru and a Lincoln Aviator, black with tinted windows."

Amazing he was able to remember so many details, I thought to myself. Trauma sends a person down one of three paths. Remembering everything.

Remembering nothing or remembering bits and pieces.

"I drove back home, took another shower, and threw away my clothes again. Got rid of the shovel and bucket. And all the shit I used to clean the car. And then I waited."

"Waited for what?"

"For whatever would happen next. I called in sick all week. Watched every newscast. Reports said he was missing. I read in the paper the club didn't have cameras. There were no leads. Few clues. And nothing happened to me. By the end of the weekend, I was ready to go back to work."

"So you go from regret to relief," I said.

"Yeah."

"How'd you come to write the article?"

"Got assigned to it. How's that for Karma?"

"Wow."

"When my editor called me, I thought it was a setup. I was freaking, thinking the police would be waiting for me there. I sat at my desk for almost an hour before leaving. Thought about getting in my car and taking a header into a tree. Had a panic attack before I got there, but when no one got in my face and I didn't confess anything, something changed."

"What's that?"

"Covering the case helped me learn what the police knew."

"Gave you an edge."

"Yeah."

"How do you feel revealing this to me?"

Luke pressed his crossed arms tighter against his chest. "Relieved, but..." His voice trailed off.

"Yes?"

"But—conflicted."

"Why?"

"That he's *there*. That his family can't rest."

"Tell me why that upsets you."

"It just does." A tinge of remorse deepened his voice. "A proper burial ends it all."

"For who?"

"Ends it for the family."

"And would that make you feel better?"

"It'd be a start," he said.

I remained quiet, hoping he'd go further with his thoughts.

"I also feel worried telling you. A part of me thinks you'll turn me in."

"That wouldn't happen," I said.

"You sure?"

"What's in the past is in the past, Luke. I told you, I'm barred from reporting it. It's part of the confidentiality pact."

"Doctor-patient privilege."

"Are you thinking of hurting yourself? Or feel an urge to hurt someone else, Luke?"

"No."

"Then your secret stays here."

Luke sighed.

"The only way to get better is to trust me and trust how therapy works—no matter what you've done."

"*You* don't feel conflicted?"

"Well, actually, I do."

"Wow, really?"

"Like you, I wish the family could know where he is. Nothing's worse than not knowing."

"It's a no-win," he said. "They don't know, they suffer. They find out, I go to jail."

"If we think of it in those black and white terms, I suppose you're right. But maybe we can find some resolutions in the grays."

"That was pretty blunt," he said eventually.

"What was?"

"Telling me you're conflicted."

"But it's the truth," I said. "Being honest is important for you. And for me. Without honesty, therapy doesn't work."

"I didn't think you'd be so real with it. I mean, you're not afraid of me. What I did and all?"

"I should be afraid because you're some kind of monster? Is that what you said before?"

"Yeah," Luke replied. "That's pretty much what I think."

"I *was* afraid of hearing what happened, the terror of it all, but I'm not afraid of *you*. I want to understand you and help you."

Luke was silent, absorbing my words.

"Sharing this isn't easy, I know," I said.

"No. And now you know what my panic is really all about."

I remained silent, feeling that his words were a powerful way to end the session.

Some patients who've been in treatment before instinctively know how time works in sessions. They can sense the end approaching. Luke was one of those patients and moved into a comfortable silence.

"Before we stop, Luke, how was lying on the couch?"

"It did make things easier to talk about."

"And your anxiety?"

"It was there, but I was able to control it better. Just like you said could happen."

"Good. We'll keep doing this. But we have to stop for now."

Luke sat up from the couch and was slow to stand. I rose as he did and walked to the door to escort him out. He was tentative as he looked at me, which I understood, given the nature of the session.

"See you Wednesday," I said.

"Bye, Dr. Reese," he replied—and was through the door and gone.

Notes

Luke Ferro killed Donald Gallin.

It was no accident. It was murder.

It was a deliberate act, violent. Luke physically beat him with his own hands. Broke his neck.

Luke had the foresight to cover his tracks—to erase his accountability when it happened—and even days later.

Transference: Luke remained positively connected to me. Layers of guilt, remorse, anxiety, worry. Shame and regret were noted in the session too.

Counter-transference: So many feelings for me. Mostly horrified and filled with terror. Traumatized by his story—felt detached and distant as I listened. Most likely from the revulsion, shock, disgust, disbelief.

But I still hold a positive connection to Luke. Want to help him.

Why do I still feel this?

Just touched my own teeth. I slid my index finger across them. It would take tremendous force for teeth to shatter. Outlined my face, tracing the arches of my brow and cheekbones, my mouth and jaw, imagining the force that crushed Donald Gallin's face.

Relevant issues: Mixture of panic and rage set off by humiliation. Did alcohol set this into motion? Would this episode of dyscontrol happen if he didn't drink that night? Did alcohol loosen his self-control?

Diagnosis: Panic Disorder. Now looking at Narcissistic Personality Disorder or possibly Antisocial Personality Disorder operating.

Prognosis: Guarded.

Monday Night

I had to get to the ocean.

I needed the sights, smells, sounds, and touches of the sand and surf.

I was in a free fall, crushed by the session with Luke.

The office was a stone's throw from the water—the singular feature that made renting here worth every penny. I dropped my things in the car and was at the beach in less than a dozen steps.

I kicked off my heels, letting the cool, wet sand to scrub against my feet and allowed the sounds of the waves and tangy salty air envelop me. It was almost nine o'clock, and the sun was inching its golden rim into the horizon. I watched as a few sailboats puffed toward the docks, done with the seafaring day, as others beamed running lights as they headed out to sea.

I walked the shoreline for nearly an hour. I replayed the session with Luke in my mind from beginning to end. Images of Luke's descriptions haunted me, but it was hard to catalogue them in any kind of clinical significance. They flashed in pieces, delivering a shudder or wince as they randomly appeared. It was then I realized how traumatic it was for me to witness his story.

I found myself also thinking about Donald Gallin's parents—and the enormous pain of them *not knowing anything*. The helplessness and hopelessness they'd be enduring must be indescribable.

They couldn't experience the comfort I felt when visiting Ryan's grave. A place I'd go to be near him. There'd never be any consolation in that permanence for Gallin's parents. What a tragedy.

Feeling the lateness of the night, I strolled back along the beach and finally sat on a bench near the parking lot. I brushed the sand from my feet and placed my shoes back on. Steve passed as I walked to my car, giving a toot on his horn. I waved back, always grateful for his presence.

I lowered the vinyl top and turned on the ignition but couldn't free my mind from the horror of the session. I reminded myself supervision with Dr.

Prader was tomorrow—and that all my flashbacks and flooding emotions would be explored there. I'd have to tolerate everything till then.

I drove home in what felt like seconds. After taking a long, soapy shower, I slipped into silver satin chemise, one I hadn't worn in months. I brushed my wet hair back into a ponytail while glancing at my silhouette in the mirror. As I clipped on a beaded barrette, I saw it in the reflection.

The unmistakable broad chassis of a black Cadillac.

I turned around and ran to the bedroom window, seeing the dark sedan turn into my driveway.

"Who the hell is this?"

I bolted from the bedroom and ran down the hallway to the front door. By the time I deactivated the alarm and unlatched the locks, the Cadillac backed out. As I flung the door open, I saw it head down the street.

As fast as I could run, I sprinted down the steps, across the grass, and over the curb, but by the time I reached the middle of the road, the car was out of sight.

"New York license plate."

I bent over to catch my breath.

"C A X . . ."

I closed my eyes, trying to remember the rest.

"Dammit."

I walked back to the house feeling defeated.

Luke drives a red car and has a Florida license plate, I thought to myself, closing the door. "Who *is* that?" I said aloud to Elvis, his tail big and bristled from the commotion.

I realized I was curious, not fearful as I'd been days ago. I wondered who I knew—friend, family or patient—that drove a similar car but couldn't think of anyone. But I was relieved knowing what I saw was real and not imagined.

Shaking off my agitation, I re-set the house alarm, determined that I needed to be more attuned to everything in my life.

But for now, I was determined not to shut down, close off, or insulate myself.

I was emerging from a long absence.

Supervision

Tuesday, June 13th

“What's this?” I said opening the door to Dr. Prader's office. “Just got here and found it all.”

Prader's desk was turned upside down revealing its gray tubular steel legs. Along the walls, diplomas and artwork were upturned, as were the photos, which sat on her credenza. Two metal chairs draped with stethoscopes sat on top of the filing cabinets, which were shifted to the other side of the room. On the floor were dozens of latex gloves.

“I guess the psych interns have revolted.”

“And this is okay?” I asked.

“It's a rite of passage,” Prader said.

“For who?”

“For them. For me. For our bonding and attachment as they go through training.”

“I enjoy a good joke, but this is kinda hostile.”

“Well, a prank is just that. Part fun. Part aggression,” Prader said. “I've been pretty hard on them. This is their way of getting me back.”

“So, this is a badge of honor?”

“Oh yes.”

“Well, it's good I don't work here.”

“This place wouldn't be a good fit for you, Alicia. But private practice wouldn't work for me.” Prader signed as she tapped the desk with her foot. “Will you help me with this?”

"Sure," I signed.

Together we upturned the desk and moved it back to its place. Spotting her white lab coat stuffed in one of the desk draws, I pulled it out with a laugh.

"Now what?" she asked.

"Apparently you're not Dr. Susan Prader, Chief of Psychology anymore."

Prader moved closer and narrowed her eyes to see the handwritten label over the embroidered left chest pocket. "Does that say *Sarah Bellem*?"

"Indeed it does."

"*Cerebellum*. Very clever."

Prader found a nearby broom and tried to sweep aside the surgical gloves, but they didn't release their rubbery hold against the tiled floor. "I'm going to have to get maintenance up here to pick them up."

"And to move these cabinets back," I said, pointing to the metal behemoths. "We'll need medical attention if we try on our own."

Prader looked around and agreed. She moved her attention to our supervision. "So, tell me about Lucas. Did you learn more?"

"Yes. It's as bad as something can get. He beat a man to death."

Prader dropped the hold she had on the broom. "Damn. I was hoping for something else."

"Me too."

"What other things did you discover?"

"He buried the body. Been having panic attacks since."

"Okay, so he feels bad about it."

"He was smart about things too. Covering his tracks, wiping away his prints. Dr. Prader, he detailed so much of the crime—I was terrified and...amazed."

"That he had such recall."

"Yes," I signed, afraid to say the word aloud.

Prader took both chairs down from the cabinets and draped the stethoscope around her neck. She motioned for me to sit down. "You feel safe in the session?" Prader signed.

"Luke's on the couch. And it seems to calm him enough to explore issues," I signed.

"Good," Prader signed. "Did you talk about the Doctor-Patient privilege?"

"Told Luke as long as he doesn't plan to hurt himself or anyone else, his disclosure's protected," I said, speaking.

"Any other violence reported?"

"I didn't get to that yet. I'll examine more next session."

"Okay, good. You need explore his early childhood," Prader signed.

"Yes, that's already part of my treatment plan."

"Good. What about you? Is there anything specific you're experiencing with this patient?" Prader asked, returning to speaking.

"Got a lot of flashbacks to the session rolling around in my mind."

"Imaging what he told you—or regarding Luke himself?"

"Visualizing what happened that night."

"Yes, well, that's par for the course. When I worked at Rikers, I didn't sleep the first three months. Things I heard were horrific."

"How'd you get through it?"

"It got easier. Less shocking over time. I used my reactions with the patients, sometimes sharing my counter-transference. Other times, I pulled the imagery as a tool to understand what the patient needed to control. Or kill off."

"I see," I said.

"You've done that before with patients, and I know you can do it with Luke. Just tell yourself to weave the frightening imagery into the psychoanalysis."

I nodded. "Oh, and there was a car again in my driveway. I got the first few letters of the license plate," I said.

"You know anyone who can do more digging for you?" Prader asked.

"Yes, the security guard at my office. Former cop. Shouldn't be a big deal for him to check into this for me."

"It's time for us to stop, Alicia. I'll put you in the book for next Tuesday." She rummaged through the mess and clutter. "That is if I can *find* my appointment book," she said. Without warning, Prader slapped her hands against her thighs, making her bracelets clang noisily together. "And where on God's green earth is the phone?"

I stood in the archway of the door and glanced again at the chaos. "This still tickles your funny bone?"

"You've no idea."

I left the hospital and headed back to the garage. The sun was hanging high in the sky, and I followed the form of my shadow as I walked. It was long and fluid and looked as if it was clipping at my heels. At first it reminded me of a puppy nipping at my heels. But as I stared at it longer, it took on a more malignant appearance.

The image became shapeless.

Amoebic.

Like a floating menace.

I suddenly felt uneasy again but made a mental note of my swirling reactions. By time I got to the Saab, the shadows were gone. And so were the feelings.

I phoned Steve as I made my way back to the office. When he didn't pick up, I left a message on his voicemail.

"Hey Steve. It's Alicia Reese. I need a favor. I'll go into it more when I see you later, but I need a license check on a car."

Tuesday Night

I put in a full day at the office, working noon till seven. It'd been a tough few days since Luke's disclosure, and I was looking forward to a quiet night. I imagined eating a late dinner of leftovers, cozying up with Elvis and reading a good book. Some P.G. Wodehouse or a Shakespeare comedy would do the trick. That's what I needed.

Just as I approached the house, something darted out in front of me.

"Holy shit."

I cut the wheel of the Saab hard to avoid it and jammed the brakes. The car stopped against the curb, scraping the front bumper. When I jumped out, I saw something on the side of the road.

"AJ—you all right?" I asked.

"I twisted my fucking ankle."

"Are you hurt anywhere else, honey?"

"I'm not your fucking honey," AJ said with a snarl.

"Well, *I'm-not-your-fucking-honey*, are you cut or bleeding?"

"No. Just my ankle," she said, wrapping her hands around her foot.

"Okay, up you go" I hoisted her off the grass. "Can you stand?"

AJ balanced herself against me and pressed her weight down on her foot. "Ow, it hurts too much."

"All right. I'll drive you back to the house."

"Great. Just great," she said hopping into the car.

"Sneaking out or sneaking back?" I asked.

AJ tossed her long, red hair back and rolled her eyes at me. "Out. Met a cute guy at the mall. Supposed to go to the movies now."

"Well, I'm really sorry this happened, AJ."

"Not as sorry as me."

"So...he's cute?" I asked, trying to shift the mood.

"Yeah." AJ cracked a small smile. "Straight-edge, smart. Different from the guys I go for."

"But don't you think a pick you up at the front door kind of date is what you deserve? Doesn't every girl?"

AJ said nothing as she twisted her lip ring with her tongue.

I pulled into the long driveway to the D'Amico's and shut the ignition off. After maneuvering AJ out of the car, she tried one last ditched effort to plead her case.

"Alicia, could you say I was visiting you and I tripped at your house?"

"No can do."

"Traitor."

AJ huffed as she unlocked the front door, and as soon as we entered the house, she pushed herself away from me. She limped toward her room cursing, and soon, the sound of a door slamming shut clipped her voice.

"Oh, snap," Isaiah said as he poked his head out of the bedroom door, hearing the commotion.

In next to no time, Melanie and Chris walked into the foyer from the kitchen.

"Alicia, what's going on?" Melanie asked.

"I, uh, don't know how to say this, but I almost hit her with my car."

"She sneaked out again?" Chris asked shaking her head.

Melanie tightened her lips and muttered something under her breath. She looked hard at Chris and left to check on AJ.

"This kid's too much to handle," Chris said to me. "Mel's just about done with things."

"Can't we keep trying, Mom," Isaiah said, grabbing Chris' hand.

"We will. But listen, I want you to go back to your room for now."

"Aw, okay." Before Isaiah left, he turned to me and whispered, "Guess it's your turn to be a broken arrow, Alicia."

"Chris, I think her ankle's sprained. She should get checked at the hospital."

"Yeah, we'll take her."

"And I damaged my car."

"How bad?"

"Scraped the bumper. I wouldn't even bother filing an accident claim, but with everything going on with AJ and the courts, maybe we need to go by the book for this."

Chris sighed. "Good idea."

"Want me to stay with Isaiah while you guys take AJ?"

"No. Mel will stay home. I'll field this one."

"I'll get my insurance card in the car – and make a call."

I looked toward AJ's room and then back at Chris.

"Again, I'm really sorry about this."

"You did us a favor. Stopped her from going who-know's-where with who-know's-who," Chris said.

"AJ was going to the movies, with a straight-edge, nice guy."

"Well, sneaking out is just another bad decision," Chris said as she eyed a car inching up the driveway. "We would've given her permission to go if she did this the right way, y'know?"

"Yeah, I hear you."

"Must be her date," Chris said.

"Well, I'll tell him AJ's not coming out tonight," I said opening the door.

"Thanks, Alicia."

I left the house and made my way down the long driveway. As I approached the car, the driver made the headlights go from full to bright. The sudden harshness flooded my sight, blinding me like a flash from a too-close camera. I shielded my eyes with my forearm and tried to blink away the glaring afterimage. It took a few seconds until I was able to see again.

Annoyed, I continued moving forward, but the headlights darkened completely, and the car started crawling in reverse.

I'm so not in the mood for this, I thought to myself.

I extended both of my arms into the air, fingers expanded, and shook my hands. The universal gesture for *wait up*.

But instead, the car revved its engine, beamed the lights on—and to full brightness again. Then it screeched away and peeled down the street.

"Dumb, stupid teenager," I said as I caught a whiff of the burning rubber.

Session Five

Wednesday, June 14th

❝Had a terrible dream last night," Luke said starting the session.

"I'm not surprised given these last few sessions. We unlocked some deeply powerful and scary things," I replied.

Dream work was a powerful tool in psychoanalysis, where unconscious fears, desires, and emotions make themselves known.

I waited for Luke to settle into resting on the couch before continuing.

"So, what was this dream about?" I asked, grabbing my notebook to take it down word for word.

"A bear."

"Go on."

"So, this bear was chasing me. No matter where I went, it found me." Luke paused, clasping his fingers against his chest and closed his eyes. "I was running in like this decrepit forest. Where all the trees were cut down. Branches, tree limbs, and leaves were everywhere. Anyway, I kept running and running. But couldn't get away from the bear. I hid, hoping it wouldn't find me. But it did."

I scribbled, trying to keep up with him.

"The bear was freakin' huge. Had these sharp claws. There was no way for me to get away. And I knew it. Then it started tearing into my skin."

Luke opened his eyes, swallowing hard.

"How does it end?"

"With the bear attacking me."

I nodded and looked at my notes. I read the dream once and then studied it again. After a while, I gathered my associations. "So, what do you think this dream's about?

"You got me," Luke said, hiking his shoulders.

Drawing out dreams can seem like a daunting task. With encouragement, patients can sometimes deepen their insight.

"You're a writer. Use your imagination."

"Well...I'm being hunted. That's pretty obvious."

"Keep going."

"And I'm trapped."

"What else comes to mind?"

"I dunno. It's violent, I guess."

I nodded. "And terrifying"

"Yeah. It *was* scary."

"And when you tried to hide, it didn't help."

Luke nodded, chewing his lower lip.

"Tell me where you feel hunted? Where you feel chased?"

Luke stared off, saying nothing.

"What about a place you can't hide?" I asked.

"I guess...here," he finally said. "I know the more I hide, the more panicked I become."

"Mmhmm."

Luke took in a few long, quiet breaths.

"What do you think the bear symbolizes?"

"I'll tell you what my first thought was. But don't laugh," he said.

"Go on."

"The Three Bears."

I widened my eyes.

"Y'know, the mother bear. The father bear. The baby. The fucking porridge. What the hell *is* porridge, anyway?"

"Boiled oats, I think. Let's stay with the bears though."

"Okay."

"Who or what comes to mind when you imagine The Three Bears?"

"My mother," Luke said plainly.

"How's your mother the bear?" I asked.

"She had these long fake nails. I forget what you call them."

"Acrylics."

"Yeah. Acrylics. Whenever she'd scream or yell, all I saw was this." Luke held out his hands, with his fingers extended, and flailed them about wildly.

"Like huge claws," I said recognizing the symbolism. "What about your father? Could he be a bear?"

"Yeah, he can. Especially lately."

"How do you mean?"

"He's pissed I'm dragging my feet about my mother's estate. Not wanting to go to the reading of the will. Shit like that. It's not a stretch to see his yelling as growling."

"Why do you think you're so reluctant?"

"I can find out what's been left, or most likely *not* left to me, without hearing it read in front of everyone. So why should I have to go?"

"So you experience pain if you go or if you don't go."

"Exactly. I'll get chewed out either way."

"Tearing into your skin. Cornered. Like in your dream."

"Yeah."

"What about here, with me? Could *I* be the bear trying to get to you?"

Luke said nothing.

"Our work here is like cutting down trees," I said. "Pressing you to talk about Donald Gallin. Cutting down your defenses?"

"I don't feel like you're a bear, pressing me. But I do feel anxious. It's me. My shit. Not you."

"So, we could throw *you* being the bear into the mix," I said, taking another analytical perspective.

"Like this Gallin thing chasing me?"

"Yes."

Luke moved into a quiet reverie.

"What about the word itself?"

"Which word?"

"Bear," I said.

"To endure something difficult."

"What else comes to mind?"

"I can't remember. Does the baby bear find the porridge *just right*?"

"No. Goldilocks finds the baby's porridge *just right*."

"Yeah. That's right. The father's was too hot. The mother's too cold."

I nodded. "What does *porridge* and *enduring something difficult* have to do with each other?"

"I dunno—maybe because things were never *just right* at home."

"Tell me what you mean."

"Every time I'd look for some kind of comfort or understanding from my parents, I'd end up wishing I never tried in the first place."

"Love and affection were difficult to find."

"Yeah."

"Sounds like you regretted looking for those things from your mother and father."

"Uh-huh."

"In your life story, the baby bear in you was burdened with loss," I interpreted. "Your absent father. Enduring the coldness from your mother."

"Not a happy ending."

I said nothing now and waited for him to continue.

"It's kinda weird I had a dream of a bear," he finally said.

"Why?"

"I didn't think of it before, but it's definitely relevant."

"What is?" I asked, inching forward in my seat.

"Every Friday in the first grade, we were allowed to bring a toy to school. For show and tell. Boys brought in action figures like He-man. Skeletor. The girls brought stuffed animals. Cabbage Patch Kids."

I nodded, encouraging him to continue.

"One Friday we brought in teddy bears. It had something to do with going to Teddy Roosevelt's—a field trip to his summer house."

"Sagamore Hill. Yes, that's not far from the office here."

"Anyway, I had to go to the Headmaster because I ruined a few of the bears."

"How did you ruin them?"

Without hearing me, he spoke again. "My mother had to come and pick me up because I wasn't allowed to go on the field trip."

"How did you ruin them?" I repeated a little louder.

Luke's eyes were closed now. He didn't answer me again. He was faraway, transfixed in a moment in time.

"I was suspended for a week. Oh man, my parents were furious. I remember, my mother hit me."

"What happened to the bears, Luke?"

He blinked heavily, clearing away the traumatic haze. As Luke floated back into the session, his hands tightened into bloodless fists.

"I cut their heads off with scissors."

Notes

Luke brings in dream, begins session thinking of the fairytale "The Three Bears." Worked dream analysis fairly well, with only a little help. Patient is very insightful. Intelligent.

Transference: Still positive, but unconscious portions of his dream suggest his connection to me could be fearful. Will explore further.

Counter-transference: Positive, but guarded. I didn't feel discomfort or worry this session, but still have concerns. I'm filled with a sense of uncertainty.

Relevant issues: "The Three Bears" is a story about privacy and the consequences of breaking boundaries. Just realizing some of the different endings of the story:

      -Goldilocks gets scared out of the house by the bears.

      -She gets attacked by the bears.

      -She gets killed and devoured on the spot.

Other things from this dream could be used to help understand the trajectory of treatment.

Is Luke like Goldilocks?

Would he run from his own psychic house?

Is he saying he might end treatment abruptly because he's scared? Like Goldilocks, could I be terrified by what else I might find as sessions go on?

Is Luke the bear and I'm in danger?

What are the consequences of breaking boundaries here in psychoanalysis?

There's much to think about here and I need to carefully sift through all of the data from this session.

Diagnosis: Panic Disorder. Narcissistic Personality Disorder with Malignant Narcissism or Antisocial Personality Disorder.

Prognosis: Still guarded.

Wednesday Night

Music was playing off in the distance as I closed Luke's file. I followed the sounds to the window, opened it, and looked down. The restaurant next door was having a party, which thinned the thoughts of bears, tearing skin, and danger. The music was rhythmic and lively. It floated here and there—and then away on the night's breeze.

I saw couples dancing on the lanai and watched their bodies move together and apart to the Latin beat. I touched my wedding ring and was suddenly filled with thoughts of Ryan. I wished he was here, if even just for a minute.

To comfort me.

To hold me.

To help me make sense of the uncertainties I felt.

I buttoned up the office and made my way to the parking lot.

"Hey Doc," Steve shouted from the security kiosk. "Got some info on that license you wanted."

"So fast?"

"Called in a few favors. No big deal."

Steve pulled out a printed sheet of paper from a folder on the shelf in the kiosk.

Got six hits on a 2010 Cadillac with New York State tags. Two are local. One's a livery company in Manhattan, and the other's a Diane Franklin in Queens County. These ring a bell, Doc?"

"No. Nothing."

"You said the car was in your driveway a few times."

"That's right."

"Y'know, The Muttontown Club is just down the road from you. Lots of events there, especially now in the summer."

I thought for a moment, nodding as I realized what Steve was implying. "You think the car's from the limo company. And it misses the road out, turns around in my driveway, and moves on."

"All those private roads by you. Easy to get lost." Steve placed his hand on my shoulder. "Remember the time I followed you home after the Saab needed a jump?"

I nodded.

"Never told you this, but as I left, I got lost and ended up in the back roads there for a while before I found my way back to 107."

"Really?" I laughed.

"Yup." Steve gave me the sheet with the license listings. "I don't think it's anything more than that, Doc. But if you see it again, call me."

"I feel better, so thank you so much for this."

"Happy to help, Doc. Safe travels home," Steve said as I got into the car.

Instead of heading home, I took the Northern State Parkway East to the Round Swamp Road exit, and coiled around the slow curves towards Huntington. I climbed the hill at Jericho Turnpike and veered left onto Oakwood Road. I'd taken this route so many times in the last few years. I could make the drive with my eyes closed.

There weren't any gates at The Huntington Rural Cemetery. Quite frankly, if you didn't have a loved one buried there, you probably wouldn't even know the place existed. It was tucked away from the tree-lined street, with mile-high hemlocks and walls of greenery.

I rolled into the entrance and parked next to the row of graves where Ryan was buried. Then I grabbed a blanket from the trunk of the car. The moon was full and beamed brightly above me, lighting my way.

Standing there, I leveled my eyes on the marble headstone. The rocks and shells I left were still there—as they always were, untouched by the elements or visitors. I pulled a peach colored Whelk shell from my pocket and set it alongside the others.

"Found this at Tobay Beach."

The grass beneath my feet was soft, and the air was warm, so I put the blanket down, sat down, and kicked off my shoes. The memories came slow at first, and then all too many at once competing for my attention. It wasn't long before a warm flow of tears streamed down my face.

I visited with Ryan for a little over an hour. When I got home, I fixed Elvis his dinner and heated up some leftovers for myself. Afterwards, I took a bath—hoping the long, hot soak might quiet my mind.

It didn't.

I dressed for bed and made Elvis sleep next to me. I was grateful he chose to stay and not run off to his own bed. He slept soundly, purring at first and then falling into a deep sleep. But I tossed and turned all night.

The morning came before sleep did.

Session Six

Friday, June 16th

"I've been angry before. Done things to get back at people, but not like this," Luke said.

"What else have you done?" I asked.

"Well, when I was eight, I locked Eleanor, our nanny, in the wine cellar. On purpose. She was there almost four hours before my parents found her."

"Why'd you do that to Eleanor?"

"Sometimes things got knocked over when she cleaned around the house. She blamed me a lot. My parents got really pissed at *me* for being careless and shit. So the next time she had to go down in the cellar, I shut the door and locked the door behind her."

"So no one knew you locked her in?"

"No. To this day, it remains a family story everyone laughs at. But I laugh for an entirely different reason."

Although Luke presented these facts in a casual way, I was taken aback by this story. This was remarkable hostility for an eight-year-old.

"Did she continue to blame you for her mistakes?"

"Yeah, but it didn't bother me as much. I just did other things to get even."

"Like what?"

"Put bugs in her bed. Moved things around so she couldn't find them. Whenever she was cruel to me, I gave it back. She didn't know, though."

"You liked fooling her?"

"Yeah."

"When else did you do things like this?"

"When my dad didn't take my side on things, there'd be days he'd *forget* to put on the parking brake in his car. Y'know, it'd roll down the hill."

"You'd arrange for that to happen."

"Yes."

Luke talking about cars made my mind think about the Cadillac again.

"You said your dad has a car collection."

"Yup. Fifteen cars. Sixteen, if he gets the DeLorean."

"What kinds of cars are in his collection?"

"Muscle cars from the fifties and sixties. I never got to drive them or anything."

"How come?"

"My dad's not a good sharer."

"What's your dad's everyday car?"

"He doesn't really have an everyday car," Luke said coolly. "He likes to rotate from his collection."

"I see."

"He's cruising around in his fifty-seven El Dorado this week, I think."

Once again, I had no reason to link Luke to the Cadillac, but it was again in my mind.

"How did revenge play out with your mother?"

"I'd take jewelry. Or her keys. Liked seeing her get bent out of shape." Luke stopped. "I used to pee in her drinks when she wasn't looking. Throw dirt in what she cooked sometimes."

It was easy for me to be silent as I was factoring in so much at that moment. I listened to Luke; his voice was steady, no sense of shame or discomfort about doing these things. It was as though the stories weren't significant to him. They weren't red flags.

It was mischief. He didn't see what I saw.

Pathology.

Disorder.

"You think a lot of children do things like this?" I asked.

"Kids do a lot of weird stuff, I guess."

"Other children do mischievous things. But not to this degree, Luke."

"You're being honest again, right?" Luke said.

I said nothing, again using silence to move the therapy deeper.

"You're right, though," he replied. "I know I was different as a kid, Dr. Reese."

Luke fell silent. Gradually, he became restless, shifting his arms and legs. Eventually, he exhaled noisily, the way one does when feeling burdened.

"What are you thinking about?" I asked, sensing he was conflicted.

"I don't how to say it because I'm already a fucking freak in your eyes."

"Remember, this is not about judgment. It's about understanding."

"I was eleven. Sixth grade. I—I took a cat and drowned it."

"Whose cat?" I asked.

"My mother's. Penny"

Hearing him say this, I felt my eyes widen and my mouth drop open. Luke was on the couch, and I was grateful he didn't see my reaction.

"Okay. Tell me what happened."

"She loved this cat. Treated it better than me. Better than anyone, really. I took it out one night and shoved it under the pool cover."

I leaned back in my chair, speechless and stunned.

"My mother couldn't find it, but she never stopped looking. When the pool opened in May, there it was floating in the water."

"She must've been devastated."

"It was gross. Never saw anything so disgusting. And after a while, I felt bad. I remember crying for days about it."

Hearing this narrative upset me more than listening to Luke describe what he did to Gallin. Within seconds, I realized this session highlighted something more troubling—a pattern of violent behavior. Killing was not a one-time occurrence. It happened before, and if it had happened at age eleven and at age twenty-five, it could happen again. There was also a sixteen-year gap to account for between Penny and Donald Gallin.

Are there more killings to discover?

My stomach pitched, and I felt lightheaded. But I had to press on.

"Sounds like you were upset you killed Penny, just like you felt regret about Gallin."

"Yeah."

"I think you take your own feelings of rage and deadness and make others suffer."

81

"How do I make sure it doesn't happen again?" he asked.

"By telling me if there's any more secrets."

It was almost imperceptible, but the barrel of Luke's chest lifted up ever so slightly and then back down in a shudder. He began to cry. I saw a tear make its way along the side of his face. His body shook silently, and then without warning, he pounded his fists into the couch cushions.

"I have these attacks because...because...I can't control my emotions... and...I'm afraid I'll lose control again."

Again. I heard him say *again*.

I regarded him closely, studying his posture on the couch.

"Have you lost control other times?"

"No, no more surprises," he insisted. Luke grabbed a tissue, wiping his eyes and nose.

"Is that the truth?" I pressed again, leaning forward in my chair. "Is that *really* the truth?"

Luke bolted up from his resting position and swung his legs to the side. I shrank back as he looked at me long and hard.

"Just can't talk anymore today," he said. "I'm gonna have another panic attack if I do."

Before I could respond, he handed me his tissue and rushed from the room.

"Luke," I shouted as I got up from my seat.

I tried to catch up to him, but the door slammed. By the time I got to the waiting room, he was already out the office suite. I moved into the building's hallway and ran toward the stairs just as the door clicked shut. I hauled it open and took the stairs, jumping onto the concrete landing.

"Luke, wait," I yelled.

My voice echoed around the walls, as did the trailing noise of his footsteps.

Seconds later, the only sound I heard was my own breathlessness.

As I walked back into the office, I heard my words again and again in my head

Is that the truth?

Is that really the truth, Luke?

My hands began to tremble, and my knees weakened.

I fell to the floor as a wave a terror took hold of me.

Notes

Luke reveals he killed the family cat at age 11.

Long-standing history of significant aggression as a child.

He's 27 now. What's happened in between these years?

Passive-aggressive stealing, hiding and infringing on others without regret. Lack of empathy and escalation of fury and rage.

Battles panic as he tells me about this. Anxiety level so high, he flees the office before the appointment is done.

Luke is intense and unpredictable.

<u>Transference:</u> Still positive. High regard for me.

<u>Counter-transference:</u> Again, feeling terrified at times in the session. Growing fearful and suspicious. Feel the need to check on his story about the cat to maintain hopeful, positive connection. But how?

<u>Relevant issues:</u> <u>Paper</u> again. First session, the bathroom cup, he works for a paper. Now he gives me his used tissue. Is he giving me his garbage?

Another theme: <u>Dirt.</u> Puts dirt in mother's food, urine in her drinks. So primitive. Talked about being covered in dirt when he killed Gallin.

Significant history of <u>fooling</u>. Even says it feels satisfying. Is he fooling me? Could all this be untrue?

<u>Diagnosis:</u> Panic Disorder. Psychopathy. Antisocial Personality final consideration.

<u>Prognosis:</u> Guarded.

Friday Night

I was told early on in my psychoanalytic training I had the temperament to work with intense cases.

I also possessed a natural curiosity to seek out the origin of pathology instead of sitting in judgment of it.

Growing up as a Coda deeply influenced the way I approached life. Having to live in-between the spaces of two worlds made me patient, compassionate, and open-minded. I was never an all-or-nothing person, a black-and-white thinker. I preferred to see the gray of it all.

And that made me a good clinician.

But no case challenged me more than Luke.

I pulled out the Miami Press article. It was a copy, not an original, though the layout, typeface, and newspaper logo looked real. With all that went on in this session, I had to verify the article. I needed it for my own grounding.

Ryan had been a professor at Long Island University, and I was always on campus using the library. I decided to access the newspaper on microfilm. There'd be no trace that way.

The campus was a short drive from my office, and within minutes, I was at the West gate entrance and parked right next to the B. Davis Schwartz Building. I trotted down to the lower level where the periodicals were housed, and after talking to Sharon, a college student who worked the night desk, I figured out how to get things done.

"So I need The Miami Free Press for the year 2015."

"I'll bring it right out to you, Dr. Reese," Sharon replied, happy to have something to do.

After about ten minutes, she emerged with the films. "Want me to help you load it into microfilm reader?"

"I got it," I said, wanting to be alone.

I worked the directional buttons on the film tray and found Luke's article.

I pulled out the copy of the one he gave in the session and compared it.

They were identical.

"Shit. It's real," I said under my breath.

I moved to the following days and weeks after Gallin's murder and read all the articles written. No leads. I also researched the months that followed. Only two articles were written saying the trail had gone cold.

"Luke told the truth," I said to myself.

I considered making copies of all the articles but doing so required a credit card.

Could be traced back to the library here.

Emailing them to myself—or anyone else I knew—was out of the question too. Could be traced.

Instead, I exited out of the reader and brought the film back to Sharon behind the desk.

I drove home relieved.

He's not fooling me.

Session Seven

Monday, June 19th

"Sorry I left early last session."

"Not your fault. I pushed too hard."

Luke was silent for a while.

"I was pissed you didn't believe me," he finally said.

"You're right to be upset. I was shocked to hear about Penny. And I pressed the issue more than I should have."

Luke stilled himself and listened.

"I was insensitive. And I apologize," I continued.

"I don't get a lot of *I'm sorry's*." Luke ran his hands over his face, rubbing his eyes. "It's—it's a nice thing to hear."

"Why's that?"

"Because you're owning your shit. You care I got upset."

"I do care."

"Well, I realize I can't get better if I'm not honest about things. But I gotta know I can tell you anything. And that you'll trust me."

"You got my trust, Luke."

"So, do you believe me when I say, no more surprises?" he asked.

"I do."

Luke nodded, and a silence fell in the room, strangely fixed and static.

"I wish I could go back and change things. Gallin, Penny. All the stupid shit I did as a kid. When I think of it all, I feel sick."

"Disgust is a good thing. That you hate what you've done is really important."

"Why?"

"Because it means you're conflicted. And wherever there's conflict, there's possibility for change."

"How do we make that happen?"

"We start linking the pieces of your rage and your actions."

"All right."

"When was the last time you felt out of control?"

"Well, about a year. When I was at Club Camber?"

"And since then?"

"Nothing I couldn't handle."

"Any panic attacks since you talked about Donald Gallin?"

"No."

"Why do you think your emotional control is better?"

"Coming clean about what I've done."

"And what else?"

Luke brought his hand to his face and stroked his chin with his fingers. I heard the friction of his whiskers against the tips of his nails. Soft sandpaper sounds.

"My mother isn't around to torture me anymore."

"Yes. And since your mother died, how's your anger been?"

"Definitely less."

"It'd be good for us to have a plan if things worsen. I'm hoping that won't happen, but if it does, we can feel confident we have a *what-if* set up."

"Like what?"

"*What if* you *do* have an urge again? *What if* you find yourself in a rage and can't control it? *What if* you can't get in touch with me right away, what should you do? Something where if you feel any impulses to hurt someone, or even yourself, gets you the help you need."

"What will happen if I call you?"

"Well, we'd talk about exactly what you're feeling and try to contain it. We can schedule an emergency session or work over the phone."

"Okay, sounds good," Luke said.

"If we can't get a handle on your urges, we'd get you to a hospital."

"Calling you or coming here isn't a problem. But if I have to go to the hospital, what would you tell them?"

"I'd explain that you're having violent impulses and that you're worried you might harm someone."

"What if they ask if I've been like this before?"

"Well, we'd tell them, yes, you've felt this before—"

"We'd *tell* them that? We'd tell them I've killed before? Are you fucking kidding me?"

"No, no, we couldn't tell them that," I replied.

Luke's agitation was intense. He looked as if he'd spring from the couch any second. He clutched his chest as it wrenched itself up and down in spastic movements. The anxiety barreled forward in seconds.

"Luke, slow your breathing down."

Like a driver preventing a car from careening off the roadway, he steered his breathing in another direction. He took long, slow breaths in-and-out in a series of successions. Gradually, his body lost its panicked rigidity. I watched as his fluttering eyes closed and the scowl on his face melt away.

"Sorry our discussion brought that attack on," I said.

"I'm not comfortable with this arrangement, Dr. Reese. I'm just not."

"You interrupted me before I could finish. I wouldn't go into specifics. I'd explain these kinds of feelings happened before, but nothing more. What's in the past stays in the past."

"What goes on in the hospital if I go?"

"They'll stabilize your mental and physical functioning, maybe introduce medication. Once you're feeling better, we'd resume sessions again."

Luke remained quiet, thinking about what I described.

"You're angry with me now," I said.

"No shit," Luke shouted.

"Do you feel an urge to hurt me?"

"No, I'm just... just frustrated. I don't wanna hurt you. I'd never hurt you, Doc. I know you're trying to help me."

"You know I'll keep all you've told me confidential. It's important you realize what I'm saying. I'm here for you. I'll work with you, I'll do all that I can to help you. But if you feel you can't work within the plan, I—"

"I can work within the plan, Dr. Reese," he cut in.

I sighed. "That's good to hear, Luke."

The session's end was but a few minutes away.

"We have to stop here, but I'll see you Wednesday."

Notes

Session finally confirms psychopathic tendencies.

Subtype of psychopathy is secondary psychopath - guilt-prone, poor impulse control, physical aches and pains, worries, driven to avoid and escape pain.

During session, had anxiety which escalated to a panic attack and successfully managed it.

Using insight to teach him about his defenses, like displacement, splitting. Will continue to do so.

Transference: still positive. Was able to expressed anger, frustration and disappointment with me – but not feeling overwhelmed or agitated to act on these impulses.

Counter-transference: Feeling in control now that emergency plan set up. Feeling hopeful but guarded regarding prognosis. Still have positive connection to patient.

Relevant issues: Psychopathic personality resistant to change. Research suggests prognosis poor. Will discuss further in supervision.

DSM V Diagnosis: Panic Disorder, Antisocial Personality Disorder.

Prognosis: Guarded.

Monday Night

Now that I had a formal diagnosis and an emergency plan, I was ready to work the case.

I knew the likelihood of change for Luke was small, but psychoanalysis could, at the very least, offer structure and safety. As long as I didn't become an object he needed to injure or destroy, devalue or dominate, the work could be done.

As I followed the arc of my thoughts, I wondered if Luke was able to gain a sense of real control since his mother was dead.

She was gone.

Fixed forever in time.

Just as I was ready to leave for the night, the phone rang. The caller ID said it was Dr. Paula Karne.

"Hi Dr. Reese. Am I calling too late?"

"No, I'm just finishing my night, Dr. Karne."

"So, Lucas finally made it to you."

She called him Lucas, I thought to myself. *Guess he never told her to call him Luke.*

"Yes. Just started working with him."

I walked as far as the landline cord would let me, balanced the phone on my lap, and sat down on the edge of the picture window. The sunset was just too good to miss.

"I wanted to know about your work with him," I said.

"We used a lot of behavioral techniques to reduce anxiety. *Realistic Thinking, Exposure Therapy.* Even tried *Virtual Reality Therapy*. Minimal improvements, though."

"That's what he reported at the intake."

"Interesting kid. I sensed he was withholding a lot, though. Didn't really talk much. But he worked hard in the sessions. It just wasn't a good fit for him."

"Well, I appreciate the referral," I said.

"How are things going in treatment?" she asked.

"It's a challenging case. If there's anything else coming to mind about your work with him, let me know."

"I will." Karne shifted the conversation. "Might I see you at the psychological association luncheon next month?"

"Haven't RSVP-ed, but I think I'll be there."

Of course, that was unlikely, but I said it anyway. Nothing I did socially since Ryan died was ever planned. If I felt good in the moment, then I'd go. More often than not, though, I never felt like going anywhere or doing anything.

"Well, I hope you come. Would be nice to see you."

I cradled the phone back in its place after saying goodbye and set it back on my desk. The clock was nearing eight fifteen, and I thought about getting home for the night.

I detailed my call with Dr. Karne in Luke's file and then slid the rest of the day's files back into their alphabetized slots. Just before I locked the cabinet closed, the phone rang.

"Hello?"

"It's Paula again. Listen, I just remembered something important and wanted to let you know."

"Okay," I said, plucking Luke's file out again.

"I, uh—it's gonna sound a little bit crazy."

"No, go ahead, Paula. With the kind of days I've been having, I doubt it'll shock me."

"When I was working with Lucas, I felt like—well, I think he was following me around sometimes."

I bobbled the phone hearing this but yanked it back up from its cord before it landed on the desk.

"What made you think that?"

"I could swear I saw him in the grocery store where I shopped a few times. I don't think he lived nearby, so that struck me as odd."

"Did you talk to him about it?"

"Actually, I didn't. To tell you the truth, I never felt comfortable working with him." Karne paused a moment before continuing. "He wasn't authentic in sessions. Didn't really reveal himself, y'know?"

"Yeah, I know what you mean."

"Well, I hope you can help reach him in ways my work couldn't."

"Thanks for sharing this, Paula. It *is* important."

Supervision

Tuesday, June 20th

"I just want to start by saying I got this ear-worm thing going on."

"A what?" Prader asked.

"You know, a song or a phrase that gets stuck in your head."

"Never heard it put that way, Alicia."

I arched my eyebrows. "Well, I think we need to talk about it."

"So, what is it?"

"*Double, double toil and trouble.*"

"Shakespeare." Prader said. "<u>Macbeth</u>?"

"Yes."

"*Fire burn and cauldron bubble.* I believe that's how the rest goes."

"*Double double toil and trouble. Fire burn and cauldron bubble.*" I closed my eyes as I recited. "Yes, that's it."

"When did this ear-worm start?"

"On the drive here."

"So you find yourself thinking about this prose as you come to supervision?"

"Mhmm."

"You think this related somehow to your work with Luke?"

I nodded. "In supervision Saturday, I told you he admitted to killing that young man."

"Oh yes, I remember it well."

I readied myself for the next disclosure. I squared my shoulders and looked hard at her.

"In analysis this week, he told me killed his mother's cat."

Prader said nothing, but blinked her eyes several times.

"I was beside myself. Disgusted."

"We know abuse of animals is common in males with rage, abandonment, and attachment issues."

"I know. And I see now that Luke is disturbed. And his previous therapist just told me she thought he was following her around."

She pressed her hands down on the desk and leaned closer to me. "Why do you want to work this case, Alicia?"

Her question didn't surprise me. I wondered the same thing. But I had time to move through the shock of Luke's narrative over the last few days. I knew the details and subtleties of the case, but Prader was only learning the facts through my recounting of the sessions.

I was in the room with Luke, which is the most important part of all.

She wasn't there to feel, sense, or know the treatability of this case.

"I know this sounds totally off. But I feel therapy *might* be able to help him."

"Didn't you just say you were *beside yourself*?"

"Well...yes, I am, but not because I'm afraid of him. It's true what he's done is terrifying, but—"

"This patient's a loose cannon!"

"I don't think so. At least, he's not right now."

Prader leaned back in her chair.

"Look, what he did was horrifying. No doubt about it. He's antisocial and a psychopath, but he's not a predator. He wants to understand his behaviors."

"I believe you. But not him," Prader signed.

"I really wanna try with this patient."

Prader looked downward a long time before any kind of assurance returned to her face. "I'll continue to supervise you on this case, but I don't have a good feeling about it."

"Good. Because, Dr. Prader, I can't do it without you."

"The minute you feel unsafe or in danger, you'll terminate treatment. Immediately, right?"

"Absolutely."

"The prognosis is poor here, Alicia."

"I know."

"Studies say only a small percentage improve." Prader considered her words before speaking again. "What makes you think he's treatable?" she asked.

"The death of his mother. She was the source of his torment."

"And she's gone now."

"Yes," I replied. "There haven't been any more urges or rages since her death."

Prader concentrated quietly as she listened.

"He's come to each session on time, is verbal and thoughtful. He wants to reduce his symptoms."

"So, you believe his mother's death neutralized the murderous urges? But how certain can you be?"

"I'm not. But I put together an emergency plan."

"Hospitalization?"

"Yes. And I'm available around the clock if he needs to call or see me."

"Good plan."

"And if I'm in any danger, I won't hesitate to call the police."

"If that happens, Alicia, his disclosures remain with you. You *cannot* tell anyone anything."

"I know," I said.

"Can you live with that?"

"I'll have to. If I want to work the case, that's the package deal."

"I don't know, Alicia," Prader said, sensing the limitations. "And what if he is stalking you? How are you going to deal with that?"

"Right now, all I want to do is stabilize the treatment plan. I'll work every piece and confront everything as it happens."

"Use analysis to trace the origins of trauma. And help him link his rage and his actions."

"Of course."

Prader sighed. "Murderous rage. It challenges us to think in ways, we ourselves, aren't used to."

"Did you see many patients like this at Riker's?"

"Oh, yes. Many. But only a couple ever really made gains in therapy."

I nodded.

"The crucial part, of course, will be to see if Lucas can tolerate therapy, learn to understand his feelings, and change his maladaptive behaviors."

"That's my goal. Develop self-awareness and self-control. Maybe even empathy."

"No small feat," she said with her left eyebrow raised.

I shifted the supervision back to the Shakespeare parallel.

"In Macbeth, Shakespeare used witches to represent the evil in the world. Witches subverted the natural order of things. They're outcasts, living on the fringe of society, shadowy and ghostlike."

"Do you think your patient possesses these qualities?"

"Yes, Luke definitely feels like an outcast with his family. And his mother accused him of failing her by not working in the family business."

"So, he subverted the natural order of things," Prader said.

"Yes."

"But the witches in Macbeth also prophesized, Alicia. They warned and cautioned Macbeth throughout the play."

"You're right."

"Maybe the witch's incantation is more of a warning for *you*.

I considered her interpretation.

"You're saying my subconscious is warning me of danger?"

"Yes," Prader said.

I closed my eyes and allowed my mind to flow into a reverie.

"Like I said, I started thinking of it driving here, but I can't figure out why."

"Did anything else unusual happen before you came here today?"

"No," I said after thinking for a moment.

"Well, let's keep this Macbeth thread on the analytic table." Prader looked at her desk clock. "We have to stop for now."

"Okay."

"And you can call *me* anytime day or night if things get dicey."

As I left the hospital and walked to the parking garage, I saw the sky was thickening with clouds. I headed across the lot, unalarmed the Saab, and threw my belongings into the passenger seat.

As I lifted the vinyl hood and clipped its bearings into place, I did it again.

Just like I did earlier in the morning.

I jammed my thumb in the bracket.

I forgot I did that earlier, until the pain reminded again.

It was then I recalled the <u>Macbeth</u> prose, linking the ear- worm to my work with Luke. And all at once the symbolism made sense.

By the pricking of my thumbs,
Something wicked this way comes.

Tuesday Night

I finished work early and grabbed a late afternoon nap but awakened with a start, feeling something wet and cold on my face.

"What the hell—" Within seconds, I realized it was Shasta. "You scared the shit out of me, Nicole."

She couldn't read my lips, but she didn't have to.

"You forgot," she said flatly.

"Forgot what?" I tried to push Shasta off, but she kept nuzzling her snout all over me, jumping on the bed.

"Dinner. You forgot me and the kids were coming for dinner," she signed.

"It's not that I forgot. I just didn't remember," I signed to her.

Nicole and I had similar features, pale freckled skin, brown eyes, and long chestnut hair, but I was a bit taller. I took advantage of my height and weight at that moment and hip-checked her onto the bed as I walked by.

"Ow." Nicole said aloud.

I took my index fingers and dotted them down my cheeks, the sign for *crybaby*.

"Any news from the police about Soraya's break in?"

"Yes," she said speaking, hoisting herself off the mattress. "But the kids can hear us, so let's sign."

Talking in sign away from the kids was a wise choice. Though Rebecca and Seth were only five years old, they were skilled Coda's. Able to play and be busy, they also listened and monitored the environment, knowing when to offer help if needed. In fact, just as silence fell between Nicole and me, they appeared.

"Aunt Alicia," Rebecca said, poking her head into the doorway, "Where are those animal puzzles?"

"Gimme a kiss first."

Rebecca gave me a peck on the cheek.

"They're in the closet by the front door, honey."

As she dashed away, Seth ran up and jumped into my arms. "I can't find Elvis?"

"Check the loft. But it's hot up there. Bring him down and play here."

Seth jumped down and headed for the stairs like a bat out of hell.

"Don't pull his tail," Nicole yelled out.

My niece and nephew were treasures. Since Ryan and I never had children, they were as close to our own. Early in our marriage, Keith and Nicole were great about letting us be a part of the twins' life. We were their god-parents, their Friday night babysitters. We also went to soccer games, karate practices, and dance recitals. That is, until Ryan got ill.

When Ryan died, only Rebecca and Seth gave me any semblance of joy. Being with them was like a magic elixir. A medicinal tonic. As I watched Rebecca settle into her puzzle and Seth bound up the stairs, I drank the moment in.

Nicole knocked into me on purpose, breaking the spell as she walked Shasta into the living room. Once there, she removed her leash and vest and put them on the couch.

It was rest time. Shasta walked over to Rebecca, scooted herself to the floor, and stretched out by her legs.

"Don't eat my puzzle," she said to the dog.

Shasta looked away and groaned. Then her body twisted and seized.

"She's doing that coughing thing again, Mom," Rebecca signed.

"I know. She did it earlier this morning. Probably too much swimming in the pool," Nicole signed back. "I'll call the vet."

Nicole and I made our way into the kitchen.

"What's the update on Soraya's house?" I asked.

"Obviously, she's upset. She asked if Keith would set up some cameras like we have at our house."

"How are the kids?"

"We didn't tell them anything about the break in. Just some stranger danger talk. Stuff like that," Nicole signed.

"Good idea."

"Detective Scott told Soraya that there weren't any fingerprints left."

"No other clues?"

"No." Nicole changed the subject. "So why did you forget our lunch today?"

"Just busy with work."

"You do three things. Over and over and over. You go to work. You go to supervision. And you make time for me and the kids. It's not enough, Alicia," Nicole signed.

I nodded, knowing she was right.

"You need more than just that," she signed. "By the way, how's that difficult case of yours going?"

"If only I could tell you about it," I signed. "But, all things aside, I do need to get out more."

Nicole moved closer and hugged me. I wanted to shut down and push her away, but I didn't. Instead, I let her hold me and I wrapped my arms around her tightly.

Suddenly, a series of heavy thumps pounded above us from the attic.

Then a high pitch scream filled the air.

It was Seth.

Nicole felt his frenzied steps within her body at the same time I heard his voice. We both ran from the kitchen.

Rebecca, though, rolled her eyes, patted Shasta on the head, and continued doing her puzzle.

"He's such a troublemaker," she said to the dog.

By the time we reached Seth in the hallway, his cheeks were flushed, and his face was streaked with tears. He was dripping with sweat.

"What? What?" Nicole signed.

Seth's hands moved so fast I couldn't read them. Then he pointed upstairs and threw his hands around his mother.

I shook Nicole's shoulder. "What's wrong?"

Nicole picked herself up and slung Seth on her hip. She spoke to me as she brushed away his falling tears. "Seth said Ryan was talking to him upstairs."

"Uncle Ryan was talking to you, honey?"

Seth nodded slowly under his sobs.

"What did he say to you?"

"He—he sc-ared me."

Nicole rubbed his chest and gave me a sideway glance.

"How did he scare you?" I asked.

"I was l-looking for Elvis. I couldn't find him. I thought he went into the closet. So I went in there and then I saw Uncle Ryan."

"Uncle Ryan was in the closet?" Nicole signed.

"Mhmm. Uncle Ryan told me Elvis wasn't in the loft. He said Elvis was outside. He told me to look out the window."

"And did you?" I asked.

"Mmmhmm. He's by your car, Aunt Alicia."

"Let's go upstairs and you can show Mommy and me."

"Noooo. I'm never, *ever* going up there again."

As Nicole comforted Seth, I walked to the side door and peeked through the blinds. There, by my car, was Elvis stretching in the grass.

Dumbfounded, I opened the door and whistled for him to come in. I turned my attention to Seth as the cat trotted in.

"It's okay if you opened the window in the loft, Seth. It gets really warm up there."

"I didn't open it," Seth replied.

"You didn't do anything wrong, honey. Elvis likes to jump from the roof to go outside," Nicole signed.

"I *didn't* open it Mommy. It was open when I got there," Seth said, insistent.

"Well, it's okay if you did open it," I said, reaching to tousle his hair.

Without warning, Seth smacked my hand aside.

"No hitting," Nicole signed.

Seth slid off her lap and clenched his fists. "I told you. I didn't open it. I. Didn't. Open. It," Seth said screaming.

And with that, he dropped to the floor in frustration, breaking apart Rebecca's puzzle with his kicks and punches. Within seconds, both kids went into meltdown mode, and Elvis bolted out of the room.

Death had a way of distorting life.

I was familiar with how the real and imagined collided. Seth was still deeply grieving, finding Ryan's loss unbearable.

I went upstairs to the loft to close the window before Elvis got out again. It was wide open to the sills. The heat was oppressive, even with the ceiling fan on. It was amazing Seth was able to stay up there as long as he did.

The closet door was open with many of Ryan's clothes scattered on the floor. By the armoire were several pairs of shoes—and on the bed was his favorite Mets jacket. Several of the photo albums were out too.

"Oh, Seth," I said gathering Ryan's things, "I miss him too."

Before a wave of grief surged, I opened the armoire, put the items back, and placed the photo albums in their assigned spot. I hung the clothing back on the rod, trying to ignore the beads of sweat that streaked down my back.

It took several tries, but I scooted the shoes with my feet back to into the closet and propped the jacket back on its rung on the door.

Seeing there was nothing else to put away, I went to close the closet door. But when I sealed it shut, a dank, cloying scent filled my nose. It was the smell of decay—of the old, the unused, and the obsolete. And the odor knotted itself in my throat.

I coughed several times but couldn't clear my lungs. With no breath moving in or out, I started to choke. The roasting heat didn't help. I became weak. Light-headed. And nauseous.

Desperate for air, I stumbled toward the open window and gasped violently, but my vision blurred, and my hearing muted.

As I fell to the floor, the closet door opened.

In the dreamlike haze before I fainted, I saw Ryan.

And then he floated away.

Session Eight

Wednesday, June 21st

"You've never worked with anyone like me, right?"

"I've worked many tough cases, but yes, never had a patient like you."

I watched for his reaction as he rested on the couch. He said nothing and showed even less. "How do you feel about that?" I asked.

"Just wondering."

"It's something new for both of us. The territory is uncharted, so to speak. But we have a plan mapped out. We have a way to keep you and others safe. And we have trust."

"Yeah."

"All of these things allow us to do good analytic work. And that's all that matters."

"I don't know if I can do this."

"Well, I'm hoping you can."

Luke shrugged.

"Your panic brought you here. And you're secrets will set you free."

"I *have* been feeling better."

"And don't lose sight of the fact since your mother died, there haven't been urges."

"Yeah," he said, absorbed in thought.

"Sometimes the hard thing to do and the right thing to do are one and the same. It's painful coming to terms with all you've done, but it's the right way to help you."

"No pain, no gain."

"In a matter of speaking, yes."

The room grew quiet, and I waited for Luke to bring something forth. When he didn't, I guided the session to a subject of importance.

"I want to talk about what was going at the time Donald Gallin was killed."

"Okay."

"What was happening with you and your mother?"

I watched as Luke closed his eyes. He folded his arms and crossed his ankles. The room was tranquil. The windows were open, with sounds of water and wind chimes filling the air. And the orange haze from the setting sun fell in slices through the blinds, their shafts of light bending on the carpet— softening his state of mind.

"My last year in college," he said, finding the timeline. "And that semester, I was really sick. Had an ulcer. Almost lost my internship."

I stayed quiet, letting the regression deepen. I didn't want to interrupt the resurrection of these memories by asking questions.

Memories link to associations. Associations link to conflict. Conflict leads to trauma. And trauma leads to answers.

That's the power of psychoanalysis.

"When I was a little kid, Eleanor would give me the empty coffee cans instead of throwing them out. I'd play with them. Hit them with spoons, like drums. I remember one time, I took one of the cans outside, and I put this big spider I found in it. I stood by the garage and rolled it all the way down the driveway. When I opened up the can to let the spider out, it kinda walked in circles, like it was dizzy."

"You were just talking about being in school and having an ulcer. Then you jump to a memory about a dizzy spider. In that last year of college, were you feeling dizzy or unable to find your way—like the spider?"

"During that semester, my parents were updating their wills. Phone calls back and forth. Conference calls with lawyers. Lotsa bullshit. My parents wanted to leave everything to me and my brothers equally with the house. The money. But I was mad about how they were breaking down the business."

"What was going on?"

"My mother wanted me to only get a small holding in the business. My brothers would get the lion's share."

"How was that structured?"

"Forty, forty, twenty."

"Forty percent to each of your brothers and twenty percent to you?"

"Yeah."

"What was the reasoning for this?"

"Well, like I said, I didn't really have an interest in the business. My brothers worked directly in it, running the whole show. My father wanted us to share the business equally, but my mother was her usual controlling self. I kinda felt it was my mother's way of punishing me since I was hell-bent on doing something different with my life."

"How did you feel about it?"

"I was pissed off."

"Your brothers feel the same way?"

"They thought it wasn't fair either. They were making big salaries in addition to the shareholding. They felt we should be even shareholders. They knew what my mother was doing."

"Sounds like it was rough on you."

"It *was* a bad time. I remember my mother leaving me messages on my phone saying she and Dad were fighting. Telling me how I was ruining the Ferro legacy. Shit like that. After a while, I'd just delete the messages the second I heard her voice. It was like she was giving me a play-by-play of *her* misery."

"I see."

"Dad would call to check up on me, but I didn't want to talk to him either. Didn't want to deal with any of it. I had such a hard time studying for classes. Even went to the infirmary a few times. They gave me some tests and they found the ulcer. I was a freakin' mess. Couldn't get to class. Missed a lot of days at my internship."

"Like the spider, you couldn't find your way."

"Stupid rich people and their fortunes. Money doesn't buy happiness. By the end of the spring semester, I was done with the bullshit. I called my parents and my brothers to tell them to just leave it forty, forty, twenty. I didn't care anymore."

Something long hidden was now surfacing. Luke's eyes fixed into an unblinking stare.

"I remember wishing my mother would drop dead. I even told her that."

"You told her you wished she was dead?"

"Yeah, I said, *drop dead you stupid fuck.* It was the first time I told her how I really felt, and it was the last time I ever spoke to her. I hated her so fucking much."

Luke was upset but in control.

"I dumped my phone and got another cell so no one could bother me anymore. I just graduated, had a job, and I didn't need anyone's money anymore. I had my own."

"So you cut yourself off from them."

"Yeah."

"How do you think this links with what happened to Donald Gallin?"

"No clue, Dr. Reese."

"You're upset with your mother, wishing she was dead. Even saying it to her. But you can't kill her off."

"But I can hurt someone *like* her. Is that it?"

"Yes," I said, moved by his insight. "You found someone to fill in for your mother."

"Gallin was in the wrong place, wrong time."

"Right."

"He was an easier target for me. Someone I didn't know. Someone I didn't care about."

"Yes."

"And how he acted reminded me of all the things I hated."

"That's called displacement. Taking something you want to do to a person—but act it out with another person."

"I get it."

"It's important we look at what happened with Penny and Gallin as part of a systematic cycle, Luke. We need to understand the psychic structures that made those things happen. It's about understanding who you were then, who you are now, and who you are becoming."

Breathing slowly in and out, Luke said nothing, but I felt he was taking in every single word I said.

"What happened to the spider?" I asked.

"I took him out of the can."

"You did?"

"Yeah—and I let him go."

And there it was.

I hoped the metaphor ignited his insight. How he was both the spider and the one rolling the can.

The abuser and the victim.

And by letting go, he abandons both roles.

I heard Luke's breathing intensify and his body stiffen and constrict. But this was different. The sputtering and huffing weren't from panic—but from the full force of catharsis.

Luke wept in waves of anguish, disgust, and shame.

It's never easy watching someone go through that.

I sat still, wishing something curative would happen in the moment.

I watched Luke sob for the remainder of the session.

And waited.

Notes

Encouraged by Luke's ability to use insight to examine disturbing experiences. Was able to tolerate comparing Gallin to his mother.

Talked about an early childhood spider/can game. I feel that this game is a metaphor for his life. Trapped. Controlled.

Continue to teach Luke about his maladaptive defenses.

Will continue to explore Luke's earliest memories in the next session.

What other traumas are there?

Would like to learn about healthy moments in his life.

Is it possible to detect when psychopathy emerged?

Transference: Still positive.

Counter-transference: Positive and guarded. But feeling energized by the clinical work. Patient is capable of deep thinking. But remember—don't let this cloud awareness that he's a psychopath

Relevant issues: Symbol of PAPER again. The final straw that pushed Luke over the edge was about shareholding, paper holding.

Dangerous behavior pattern unfolds in the following way:

- Humiliation and/or ridicule = collapse of the self.

- Then rage evolves into need for complete annihilation of the person responsible for setting into motions these experiences.

Prognosis: Guarded, but hopeful.

Wednesday Night

I was so pleased with how Luke's session went, I decided to treat myself to a dinner at Walls Wharf down the road.

I thought about getting a table outside by the water and ordering some Firecracker Shrimp and a glass of East End Sauvignon Blanc from the Jamesport Winery.

On the weekends during high season, you couldn't get near Walls. But it was a Wednesday night. And if by some chance I was wrong about it being slow, I'd get my meal and sit on the beach itself. They did that sometimes for the locals.

Before closing the office, I phoned Dr. Prader to touch base.

"Dr. Susan Prader," she answered.

"Dr. Prader? What are you doing in the office so late? I expected to get your answering service."

"Started teaching a workshop in my office on Wednesdays for the Postdoc Institute—and just finished up," she said. "Everything okay?"

"I was going to leave you a message that my session with Luke went well."

"So very, very good to hear that, Alicia,"

"Listen, I won't keep you. I'll see you next week for supervision."

After ending the call, I gathered my belongings, locked up the suite, and took the elevator down to the ground floor. The building, as usual, was unoccupied at this hour, but I knew Steve would be somewhere making his rounds.

Before getting into the Saab, I made another quick phone call.

"Hi, Mel. It's Alicia."

"Hey there. What's doin?"

"I'm getting home a little late tonight—and I was wondering if Isaiah would feed Elvis?"

"Actually, 'saiah is out with Chris at a Mets game. But I'm home here with AJ. She and I can go over and take care of that."

"Great. His kibble's in a bin on the counter."

"You mean the one I've seen a hundred times that says *Cat Food*?"

"Yes, smart ass. And don't let Elvis talk you into giving him a second scoop. He gets pushy when I'm not around."

"Okay, I will."

"Thanks, Mel. Appreciate it."

"Nice to hear you're going out, Alicia."

"Yeah, well, it's only dinner by myself. Let's not get carried away."

"Baby steps, my friend," Melanie said.

"Speaking of baby steps, how's things with AJ?"

"The brace on her ankle slows her down, which is good because she's still grounded."

"How's she doing with that?"

"Pretty good. She tests me and Chris, but for the most part, she seems to be in good spirits. AJ's talking with this new guy a lot on the phone. When I hear the conversation, it sounds sweet. No bad language or plans to ditch the rules here. They talk about video games, movies, and things like that."

"Sounds really great, Mel. Maybe all your limit setting and loving concern is making a difference."

"Wouldn't that be something," she said before hanging up.

I slipped into the car, cranked the ignition, and pushed the gearshift into drive. I passed Steve as he looped around the security kiosk and tooted my horn.

He honked back.

I turned onto Main Street and headed north toward Greenwich Avenue with a flicker of hope in my heart. It was such a good day.

And it would be a good night.

I was sure of it.

Session Nine

Friday, June 23rd

"Dr. Reese, I—I did it again."

"What? Did what?" I asked, blinking the sleep from my eyes.

"Ohmygod. I think she's dead."

I bolted upright, no longer in a dreamy haze and turned on the nightstand lamp. "Who's dead?"

"She—she's not breathing."

"Jesus, check her pulse."

Over the phone, I heard whooshing and crackling sounds.

"Nothing. I got nothing."

"You said you'd call before things got bad." I jumped out of bed. "*Before*, goddammit, *before*."

"I fucked up. Please. You gotta help me."

"Where are you?"

"Cantiague Park—by the woods."

"I'll be right there."

Though it was only minutes after, I was still bound to protect Luke.

I could not break privilege.

But I did.

I changed the timeline.

"This is 911, what is your emergency?"

"I'm Dr. Alicia Reese. A patient of mine he's—he's with a woman. Says he's going to kill her."

"Is your patient with you now?"

"No, he's not here. He's at Cantiague Park." I put the call on speakerphone and scrambled to put on clothes.

"Okay, Doctor, what's your patient's name?"

"Lucas Ferro. F E R R O." I laced up my sneakers, getting ready to go.

"Who's he with?"

"I don't know. A woman. He told me he's with a woman."

I grabbed my keys and left the house. I ran to the car, opened the door, and flung my handbag in the passenger seat. I secured the cell phone in its carrier on the dashboard, not even stopping to connect the Bluetooth—and seconds later raced out of the driveway.

"He's at Cantiague Park?" the dispatcher asked.

"Yes! Check the wooded areas," I said, flooring the car's gas pedal.

"First responders are on route and we're alerting Park Security. Doctor, describe your patient?"

"Twenty seven. Black hair, blue eyes, muscular build, about six feet."

At this late hour, Route 107 was empty, which was good because my driving reached breakneck speeds.

"You're at 917-555-0344?"

"Yes, yes, my cell. I'm on my way there."

"Doctor, stay on the line."

"I will," I said and whipped around a curve in the road.

I flew past the 106 merge, going through red lights and blowing past slower cars on the shoulder. Taking the fork by the Broadway Mall, I clipped a traffic sign, knocking it out of the ground.

"I'm almost there," I said to the dispatcher.

"We have cruisers on the grounds, Doctor."

The mile to the park felt so out of reach, so far away.

Suddenly, a police car whizzed by with sirens blazing and red lights pulsing. I followed behind it and increased my speed.

"I'm behind car 214," I said to the dispatcher.

"Okay, I'll let them know."

In seconds, I saw the officer's right hand rise up to wave in the rearview mirror. Together, we rocketed the rest of the way, turning sharply at West John Street and again into the park entrance.

As we screeched to a halt in the parking lot by the hockey rink, two detectives emerged from the crowd.

"Dr. Alicia Reese?"

"Yes."

"I'm Detective Skolnik. This is Detective Lombardi."

I shook their hands.

"Tell me why we're here," Lombardi asked, leading us away.

"Got a call from a patient. Said he was gonna hurt this woman."

"This a dangerous patient of yours?" Skolnik asked.

"We wouldn't be here otherwise."

"Right," Skolnik said. "This patient got a name?"

"Lucas Ferro."

"What about the girl?" Lombardi said.

"I don't know anything about her. He's in the park. In the woods somewhere."

Skolnik and Lombardi looked at each other non-plussed. Without warning, their walkie-talkies blared out. "Got some clothes over by the golf course. Hole five," a voice said.

"Copy," Lombardi replied.

The three of us took off on foot. The golf course was dark, but we ran down the pavement toward the first tee using the distant beams of the searchlights as a guide. There was chatter from the walkie-talkies, but I couldn't make out what was being said. I just wanted to keep up with the detectives.

The greens were wet from the muggy summer air, and my feet were soaked by the time we reached the second tee. As we closed in on the second hole, we cut across the fairway along with several other officers who fanned out in different directions.

The shortcut took us right to the fifth hole. Breathless and sweaty, I followed as the running slowed to a stop. Near a sand trap by the woods, beams of flashlights gathered together. Four officers circled around something, and as I got closer, I saw a body.

I moved down the hill to see more, but Detective Skolnik motioned for me to stop. He spoke into his walkie-talkie, and a second later, a police officer was at my side, inching me away from the scene.

"Lady, you gotta move back," the officer said, pressing his hands against my shoulders.

I stopped in my tracks.

Stepping back actually improved my line of vision as the ground sloped upward. I was grateful for the distance placed between me and the body lying there dead in the woods. I needed the space to deal with my own revulsion.

At first glance, pieces of her face were missing, bitten out, it seemed to me. I turned away to hold myself together.

I looked again, this time longer, taking in details.

There were scratches all over her face and neck. Her mouth was bloody, and her eyes were black sunken sockets. Her torso was covered with patches of dry grass and leaves—and her bare legs, spattered in blood, looked shiny and wet in the reflection of the lights.

It was hard to piece it together, but a dull feeling of recognition grew.

I noticed the red hair.

Then the lip ring.

AJ?

I stifled my screaming with my hands.

It's AJ!

And as I looked for a third time, the sting of tears filled my eyes.

Oh my god, AJ. Why? How?

I threw my hands over my face as the terror exploded.

I couldn't think, speak, or move.

Slowly, my strength returned.

This is different. A sexual component.

How wrong I was to think Luke's mother's death reduced his cruelty.

I rubbed my eyes trying to understand how AJ and Luke crossed paths. But a ruckus heightened in the distance.

"Suspect in custody," said a voice from the officer's walkie-talkie.

I ran toward the circle of lights, surprising the officer watching over me. In a few strides, though, he was able to grab my shoulder and pulled me to a stop.

"Ma'am, you can't go there."

"I need to see him."

"No way, Ma'am." The officer led me off in another direction. "I'm taking the doctor to the parking lot," he said into his shoulder, squeezing the buttons with his thick, strong hand.

"Copy," a voice replied.

"I'm Officer Conrad. We're going back to your car. You can sit there."

I felt defeated. "All right," I said.

Moving away from the sights, sounds, and brutality allowed me to slow my heart and catch my breath. Conrad said nothing and accepted my need to brace myself against him as we walked to the car.

As we passed the ice rink, several officers and park security milled about. Their chatter stopped as we approached. When my eyes met theirs, I saw disgust looking back at me.

And so it begins, I thought to myself. *The doctor whose patient killed a woman. The doctor who failed.*

I lowered my head and wiped my eyes. Conrad opened the passenger door to the Saab, and I slumped into the seat. Through the open window, I heard more jokes, their way of dealing with unspeakable trauma.

"The Mauler."

"Golf Course Killer."

There was more, but I didn't hear it. I was lost in my own thoughts.

I rolled back against the padded headrest and thought about the shame I felt. Not from the awkward glares of the officers. Or the things they said.

It was the shame I felt after I got the call from Luke. How I lied and changed the timeline. I took the truth and turned it against Luke—and it was life altering.

I heard a commotion and looked out the back window. Skolnik and Lombardi were walking across the parking lot. Behind them, a wall of police escorted Luke. His hands were cuffed. His white shirt was blood-soaked, torn and ripped. His face was covered with dirt and mud.

Dirt again.

Luke's eyes were blank and offered no resistance as the officers walked him to a waiting cruiser.

No resistance, until he saw me out of the corner of his eye.

Luke broke free and ran towards me. The officers charged after him, and within seconds tackled him to the ground. Detectives Lombardi and Skolnik joined the scuffle, picking him up from the pavement and throwing him hard against the trunk of the Saab. The jolt made me coil further back in my seat.

"I'll kill you. I'll fucking kill you, Reese!"

I watched in shock as everyone restrained Luke, crushing their body weight on him until he couldn't move.

"You fucking bitch," Luke screamed through a bloodied mouth.

Skolnik and the officers shoved him away and then into the back seat of the cruiser. A second later, Lombardi rapped the top of the car with her hand, signaling the driver to leave.

The car sped off in a glare of red and white lights as Officer Conrad motioned for me to come out. "You okay, Ma'am?" he asked.

I nodded.

The detectives made their way back to me.

I knew I had to be strong and convincing.

I knew nothing would ever be the same again.

Notes

Luke killed AJ.

She was beaten, stabbed and possibly strangled. Left her naked in the woods. Did he rape her?

He called me after it happened. AFTER.

    But I lied. Changing the timeline so I could invoke "Duty to Warn."

    Why the hell did I do that?

    I can't un-ring this bell.

    I have to maintain the lie no matter what.

<u>Transference:</u> Negative. Furious. Outraged. Trust forever broken.

<u>Counter-transference:</u> No longer feel connected in any way to this patient. I'm Angry. Shocked. Disgusted with myself.

<u>Relevant issues:</u> <u>Dirt</u> again. All over his face and body. Left AJ in the dirt.

I need to ask myself so many questions –

Why did I betray Luke?

Was it my own need not to witness anymore death?

Was it the realization he couldn't be helped?

Was it a moment of weakness? A moment of strength?

<u>Prognosis:</u> Poor.

Friday Morning

I barely slept and woke to the morning calls of the robins in the scrub oak trees.

Bleary eyed, I went into the kitchen to my briefcase, took out the file on Lucas Ferro, and walked over to the soapstone stove in the living room.

I opened the dual swinging doors and placed the file in between two logs that were in the hearth. Finding the matchsticks, I struck one against the bottom flint in one heavy-handed stroke. I directed the flame to the outside corners of the file and watched the heat consume the rest. I closed the metal doors, sat down on the sofa, and watched the ends curl and blacken.

Luke's clinical notes were locked in my office, as were all my patient files. Clinical notes included date of birth, phone numbers, addresses—and clinical information like dates, session times, fee arrangements, diagnoses, and treatment approaches.

Other things I felt or thought went into personal notes. It's common practice for therapists to have *shadow files*. These notes were my way of keeping track of the many psychoanalytic elements I used in treatment. How I felt. What I thought. And other reveries I experienced with patients.

These shadow files don't fall under the umbrella of a subpoena, but that didn't matter much to me right now. I wanted everything I felt about Luke to burn away into nothingness.

The breaching of confidentiality wasn't a criminal act, but it had legal and ethical implications. In the legal context, the information gathered from a breach could be challenged and usable in court.

Legally, a patient could sue a psychologist in a civil court, collecting monetary damages for the breach.

And in the ethical context, any violation of the standards surrounding confidentiality would result in expulsion from the American Psychological Association—and the loss of your professional license to practice.

Luke would learn in the discovery process of his criminal proceedings that my clinical notes had no damaging data. No mention of the murders. Just the required notations. And I'd find a way to make sure Luke wouldn't risk filing a suit against me. I didn't know *how* I'd do that, but I knew that some way, I would. Doing so, there'd be no worries about the local, state, and national psychology associations finding out about my misconduct.

Dr. Prader, though, would be disappointed when she discovered the truth. Her responsibility wouldn't involve reporting me to anyone either though. Supervision is protected by confidentiality and privilege too. But I couldn't wait till Tuesday to tell her.

I got up, grabbed the telephone, and dialed her number. It was early, and I knew her answering service would pick up the call.

"Dr. Susan Prader's Office. How can I help you?"

"I need to leave a message."

"Who's calling?"

"Dr. Alicia Reese. Tell Dr. Prader I'm okay. She'll know what that means. And I'll see her Tuesday."

After hanging up, I fell back onto the sofa and thought about AJ. I wondered how Mel, Chris, and Isaiah were holding up through it all.

And then I thought about AJ's parents.

Pressing the speed-dial, I waited for someone to pick up the phone at the D'Amico's. After six rings, the answering machine kicked in.

"Mel, Chris, this is Alicia. Please call me on my cell. Doesn't matter what time."

I closed my eyes as my mind raced to Luke, his rage and fury. What I did to him was worse than his mother—or more than any other person in his life.

His mother was a dismissive, rejecting, and insensitive person. But she was *predictable*. He knew her walk and talk. Being able to know that someone behaves in a constant way gives you a sense of structure. And an edge. You can protect yourself from people like that.

But when someone is unpredictable, the template for certainty is lost. There's no consistency. And if you trust someone like that—and then they betray you—the trauma is deeper.

I was now an unpredictable character to Luke, and in many ways, I surprised myself.

I turned on my side, curled my knees to my chest, and stroked my hair. I thought of AJ, and I ached for her. For her family. For Mel, Chris, and Isaiah. I cried long and hard.

And in between my sobs, I watched the fire glow.

Soon there'd be nothing but smoldering embers.

Brookville

Saturday, June 24

I waited until noon to start making my phone calls to cancel sessions for the week. I was in bad shape—depressed. Anxious. Overwhelmed. There was no way I could work.

Luke's crime could become a high profile case, and I needed to figure out how to talk about this with my patients. But for now, I'd tell them I needed to cancel for "personal reasons." At the next appointment, I'd discuss the reasons why—that is, if I had to. This approach allowed time to judge whether the media took hold of the story or if it fell under the radar.

Just about a half an hour into my calls, the doorbell rang several times in a row. Then there was a rapping on the front door. The suddenness filled me with anxiety.

I hung up the phone and remained still for a moment. From a space in between the blinds, I saw a dozen or so reporters and news cameras in the front yard.

"Damn."

I retreated to the loft, grabbing Elvis as I made my way up the stairs. The doorbell rang again and again. Then the knocking continued.

I ignored everything and turned on the television to the local station. The newscast was reporting the weather. The lead stories had already been covered. While waiting for the next broadcast at the top of the hour, I grabbed my phone and Facetimed Nicole.

"Hey you," Nicole signed.

"Hi. You see the news yet today?"

"No, why?"

"I need to tell you something," I signed back. "Remember that difficult case I have?"

Through a flow of tears, I signed to Nicole everything that happened—just as I had told the detectives. I couldn't tell Nicole the truth. That I'd lied about the timeline. It's not that I didn't trust my sister. I did. There was just so much at stake. And I didn't want to burden her. Nicole was there with me through Ryan's illness, and his death took a toll on all of us.

Just as I reached the point in the story where the police took Luke away, the top news stories were about to air again.

"Channel 12, now," I signed.

Together, Nicole and I watched the lead story, which featured AJ's murder. Videos of the park, the golf course, and Luke exiting the police cruiser at the precinct aired throughout the report. The story aired comments from the Nassau County District Attorney and reactions from Mr. and Mrs. Sheridan, AJ's parents. Also covered was the Ferro family legacy and their prominence in society in New York City—and then my name and a picture of my office building appeared.

"SHIT," Nicole signed and narrowed her eyes as she looked at me through the phone.

Next on the screen was Dr. Maxwell Marcus, the current president of the Nassau County Psychological Association. He explained the Tarasoff Case for viewers, saying how important its edicts are to uphold—that it's mandatory for a therapist to call the police if a patient plans to harm another person.

Seeing Dr. Marcus deepened my guilt about what I'd done. He wouldn't have agreed about the path I took.

Just before the coverage ended, the camera moved back to the news anchor who said a plea of not guilty was entered at Luke's arraignment and he was remanded without bail.

I stared at the phone, waiting for a response from Nicole. She was out of the frame, but I heard background noises of her moving around. After a few moments, she moved into view again and finger spelled "n-e-w-s-d-a-y."

Nicole held up the cover page of the paper for me to see.

"Holy Christ," I said aloud, seeing the bold headline and the photo of Luke.

Nicole turned the phone towards her television. "Channel 4," she said.

I pushed the remote to channel four. Then channel seven, and the rest of the New York stations. They all led with the murder.

"I need to get out of here," I signed to Nicole.

"Yes. Hurry," she signed.

I shut down Facetime and turned the television off. I ran down the stairs and encouraged Elvis to follow alongside.

Desperate to run away from everything, I rushed into the bedroom and slid open the closet, found my duffle bag, and unzipped it on the bed. In the kitchen, I grabbed four cans of cat food, some emergency cash, my briefcase and pocketbook—and carried them back to the bedroom. I threw in everything the bag, as well as a few days of clothing and made my way to the hall closet. Once there, I took out the pet carrier and scooted Elvis in it.

Ready to go, I walked past the foyer towards the side of the house. I moved the blinds, ever so slightly, to see if anyone was near my car. From my vantage point, I saw that no one was at The D'Amico house across the street.

The media doesn't know AJ was in foster care, I thought to myself.

As I looked further, vans were situated on the street, but one of them was blocking the driveway. There were shadows by the front door but no one by the side of the house. I'd get to the car with a good head start.

I slung the duffle bag over my right shoulder and picked up the pet carrier with my left. With the alarm set, I quietly opened and shut the side door. But then I bolted to the car and flung the duffle with a heavy swing. As I sat down, I put Elvis in the passenger seat.

The reporters by the front door heard the car start. From the rearview mirror, they ran in my direction. Their movement made those news crews in the street rush towards me. As quickly as I could, I put the car in drive and floored the gas pedal. I drove forward, past the garage, around the backyard and to the far side of the house—hoping when I reached the street, there'd be no one there.

And there wasn't.

And for a brief moment, a smile curled along my lips having outsmarted them.

The Saab bumped and jostled on the grass. Just before getting to the street, the back end carriage scraped against the curb.

"C'mon. C'mon," I said, swerving a few times before getting control of the car.

I took the back roads to Nicole's and thought about how weak I felt.

I had no appetite.

Barely slept.

I was beat up and broken inside.

Luke was likely feeling the same things, but I didn't let myself think more about that. What haunted me most were the images of AJ, murdered in the woods.

A sharp pain hit me in my stomach as I turned toward Huntington. I leveled my hand on my belly, pressing down to ease the cramping spasms, but it was no use. Sadness, terror, and guilt wrangled within me—and it was rightly so that I was in pain.

Luke couldn't have met AJ by coincidence.

My working with Luke allowed him to cross paths with her.

I was responsible for her death.

Goddammit. I should've just stopped working with Luke, I said to myself, looking in the rearview mirror. *Prader tried to talk me out of working with him.*

"Oh, AJ," I cried out. "I'm so sorry."

Supervision

Tuesday, June 27

D r. Prader knew what happened with AJ's murder because it was all over the news. What she didn't know was how the truth really played out. And I was unsure how she'd take my transgression.

"Alicia, this is so terrible. You said everything was good with this patient."

"Everything *was* good, then."

"What happened?"

I took my eyes away from hers and lowered my head. I didn't know where to begin, how to tell her what I'd done. I was at a loss for words.

Prader reached out her hand across the desk and touched my arm. "I know how hard you wanted to make this one work, but it's apparent he wasn't treatable," she said.

"I know."

"The best we can do in our line of work is to offer the possibility for change. It's up to the patient to take that further."

I tried to control my reeling emotions, but tears flowed out of me.

"It's all right," she said, handing me a tissue.

I choked on my words in-between breaths, ultimately saying nothing.

Prader brought her index finger to her mouth and crossed both hands together at the wrists. Then she dropped her arms slowly and gently back to her sides. This sign has many meanings:

Quiet.

Be still.

Peaceful.

After a while, I was able to find my voice.

"Susan, I told the police a lie." I rarely called Dr. Prader by her first name, and when I did, it was usually at a most pressing moment.

"A lie?"

"Luke called me *after* he killed AJ."

Prader's eyes narrowed as she thought about my words. "You're saying you found out after-the-fact?"

"Yes."

"Your patient did *not* call you to say he was thinking of hurting someone. He called you *after*?"

"That's what I'm saying. When Luke called me, I realized therapy would never help him. So I lied to the police. I changed the timeline."

"But you violated privilege, Alicia. You'll lose your license when this gets out." Prader rubbed her forehead as another consideration raced into her thoughts. "Luke's lawyers will eat you alive."

"I'm not worried about that."

"Alicia, you're not thinking clearly. This is a terrible error in judgment. You're going to lose everything. Haven't you lost enough?"

"Stop. Enough," I signed fast and hard. "I know this is bad. But, I have nothing to lose."

"Alicia, how can you think you'll lose *nothing*?" Prader signed.

"If you can hold my confession in confidence, no one will ever know that I lied," I signed back. I looked hard at Prader. "And Luke isn't going to tell anyone anything," I said moving back to speaking.

"You haven't been able to control this patient from day one, and suddenly you're an expert on what he *is* and *isn't* going to tell?" Prader asked.

"I know what you're thinking—the right thing would've been to stop treatment with Luke. But I didn't do that, Susan. I made the decision to stop *him*."

Prader remained quiet, and the silence stretched out painfully. She turned away from me, swiveling her chair to the side. I couldn't read her body language, and I worried if she was responding in disgust or if she just needed space to think things through.

Dr. Prader was like a loving, wise mother to me. Not only was I admitting the truth to my mentor, but I felt the shame of disappointing a cherished parent.

"How do you know Luke won't tell his lawyers about your breach?" she signed,

"I don't want to involve you more than you already are. Just know I can keep myself safe," I signed back.

Prader moved closer and spoke in a serious tone. "My responsibility as your supervisor is to tell you that you need to rectify this matter—and to make certain it never happens again. If you assure me of that, there's no need for me to go outside of this room."

"It won't ever happen again," I said. "You can count on that."

"You called her AJ. You *knew* this girl?"

"She lived across the street from me."

"What?"

Prader sat back in her chair, lifted her glasses to her head, and rubbed her eyes. As a stillness set in, I realized the worst was over. I was able to tell my beloved mentor and friend this terrible secret.

"Take away all the rights and wrongs, the professional do's and don'ts, and I'll tell you what I really think." She leaned forward and put her glasses back on. "I understand why you did this, Alicia. I don't agree with it, but I can make sense of it."

"I'm gonna slow things down in the office, refer patients out," I told her. "Maybe close my practice."

"Wise decision."

"I'm also going to stop coming here—at least until things settle with Luke's case."

"I don't think stopping supervision is a good idea."

"I'm making a unilateral decision about this, Susan. I'll be back, but not right away."

I saw a tension build in her shoulders and then slowly release as our eyes met. "I'm worried about you. And about your professional future. You can't navigate all of this on your own."

"I know what I need to do."

"Then, I want you to think about resuming analysis again."

"I'm not going back into therapy right now. I have to get through this my own way."

"Well, why don't we spend the rest of the session processing what happened with this case?"

"No. I came today to explain what I did. You deserved to know the truth."

Prader rose from her chair and moved around the desk toward me. She took my hand and held it tightly, lifting me from my seat until I stood beside her.

"All of us are much more human than otherwise," she whispered. "We're imperfect. Flawed."

And as she embraced me, I heard her bracelets jangle in and around my ears.

I held her a long while knowing when I let go, I'd be losing so much.

I was already missing her as I drove back to Brookville.

Huntington Village

Saturday, July 1

C hris and Melanie planned to spend the morning at Heckscher Park while Isaiah was in day camp. I decided to meet them there—away from the news vans and chaos on the block. I'd been keeping a low profile, staying at Nicole's, so the change of scenery was healing.

But sometimes a series of horrifying images flared like a machine gun in rat-a-tat speed.

AJ's mangled face.

Sunken dead eyes.

Bugs crawling on her remains.

Other times, just one scene flashed over and over in my mind.

The moment Luke saw me in the Saab.

And though it'd been days since it happened, I still felt the scorch of his rage.

I was worried about returning to a park so soon after AJ's murder, thinking the similar setting would lead to even more flashbacks. Before I left Nicole's house, I popped a dose of Xanax from an old prescription I had when Ryan was ill. Back then, I took it when I felt panicked and helpless —when death threatened the only world I'd known. Now, in another state of ruin, the bitter taste of the pill sickened me.

"Going to the park now," I signed to Nicole, finding her in the backyard.

"Okay. Take care," Nicole signed. She walked up to me and hugged me hard. "Call if you need me."

I smiled, grateful.

Nicole was my rock. Always was, always would be.

Turning my attention to the kids who were in the pool, I teased, "Don't turn into fishies before I come back."

The shrill of their laughter lightened the moment for a second.

"Buh-bye," they said twin-like and returned to splashing water at each other.

Shasta, who was resting in a shady spot, usually sent me off with a lift of her head. Instead, she whimpered as I walked by.

"Sick again?" I signed to Nicole.

"Vet says no. Everything's fine," Nicole signed back.

I leaned down and patted Shasta's head gently. I walked to the gate, unlatched the lock, and clicked it closed just as Shasta fell back asleep again.

The trip to the park allowed the medication to kick in, and I counted on nostalgia to bolster my soul. Heckscher was a favorite destination for my family when I was growing up. It was situated in the north coast town of Huntington—nearly seventy acres of grassland surrounded by water, brilliant flowers, and outdoor art.

As a child, I loved the playground as well as the small pier where the swans and ducks gathered. Nicole loved going into the museum on the park grounds, and my parents loved to view the seasonal blooms that lined the walking paths. As I got older, we visited less, though we always made sure to attend the annual Tulip festival and catch the National Theatre of the Deaf at the Harry Chapin stage when they were in town.

Just as beautiful as I remember, I thought walking in the entrance.

The meadows that bordered the property stretched out in the distance like lush emerald carpets, and glorious flowers tinged the air with a sweet, floral scent. I strolled down the walking path toward the playground pavilion, listening to the sounds of children's laughter with each step. I noticed how the old stone bridge and the gazebo were still in one piece—and how regal the Museum looked in the midst of the landscaped grounds.

"So far, so good," I said, cheering myself on.

As I walked further, a loose-limbed feeling settled in, and I felt my worries lighten. I thanked the side effects of the Xanax as I strolled to the pond. Soon I saw Chris and Melanie tossing snippets of bread to a pair of geese and their goslings wading in the water.

"Alicia," Chris called, catching my presence out of the corner of her eye. I raised my hand and I headed toward them.

"How are you?" Chris asked, hugging me hard as we met.

Before I had a chance to answer, Melanie leveled her eyes to mine and asked, "You doin' all right?"

"Could be better. But how are you all doing? Jesus, this has been so horrible."

Chris and Melanie looked at each other. Their sunken eyes and sloped shoulders told me they were faring just a well as I was—which was terrible.

"So much I wanna talk about...but I don't even know where to begin," I said.

Chris sat next to me and rubbed my back in soft circular strokes while Melanie stood in front of us, wiping away stray tears.

"First, tell me, how's Isaiah?" I asked.

"He's fine," Chris said. "Don't you agree, Mel?"

"Yeah, he's doing okay."

"We actually decided to keep AJ's murder away from him for now," Chris finally explained.

A long pause set in.

"Why's that?" I asked.

"A lot of reasons, Alicia," Melanie said. "He wasn't around when the media came by, and no one in the neighborhood besides you, knew AJ was living with us."

"The press hasn't made the foster care connection," Chris continued.

"But what about the police?" I asked.

"They showed up twice. Each time when Isaiah was in camp," Chris said. "And they said they'd work with us to minimize any future exposure to him."

"What *have* you told Isaiah?" I asked.

"We said AJ went back to live with her parents," Melanie said.

"Isaiah's just so young," Chris said.

"We thought it'd be traumatic to explain it," Melanie said.

"Have the police told you how AJ and Ferro knew each other?" I asked.

"The Computer Forensic Unit told us they talked and texted," Chris said.

"He was this *straight-edge, nice guy* AJ said she met at the mall," Melanie said.

Nice guy, I thought to myself.

"The detectives working the case said they met a few weeks ago at the mall. Got video of it," Chris said.

"But they didn't meet by chance," I said. "That's not possible."

"Yeah, I agree." Melanie thought further. "Was Ferro stalking you?"

"Considered that," I said. "Even followed him home to see if his car was there when I had that feeling."

"And was it?" Melanie asked.

"It was. I'd been seeing this Cadillac at work and here at the house." I stopped for a moment to recollect the images. "You guys ever see a long black caddy here in the neighborhood?"

Melanie and Chris shook their heads.

"That night where you almost hit AJ as she sneaked out, that must've been him," Melanie said.

"I never saw who was driving—or the color of the car. The brights flew on and off," I said.

"It was a red car. I saw it when it sped off from the window," Chris said looking at Melanie.

"Ferro drives a red Porsche," I replied.

"Yeah, it was a Porsche, for sure," Chris said.

"Guess he was making sure I didn't recognize him by flashing those lights."

"Jesus, he was right there. Right our house," Chris said.

"I feel so awful…" My voice trailed off. "His working with me—how could I know AJ was in danger?"

"You couldn't, Ali," Chris said.

"He was a bad, bad guy," I said, drifting off. The Xanax in full effect now, muting my sadness and my remorse.

We sat for a while in the quiet, each of us tearful and lost.

"We thought we'd grab lunch at Prime. Catch up on things," Melanie said, breaking the painful silence.

"I'm terrible company," I said.

"No, you have to come," Chris said.

I shook my head firmly. "Go have a nice lunch. Count your blessings. I'll take a raincheck." I looked back where Melanie and Chris were feeding the goslings. "Got any more bread?"

Melanie reached into a tote and pulled out a plastic bag. "Just cheerios left. They really like them."

"Thanks, I'll spend some time here before going back to Nicole's."

I walked toward the pond as Chris and Melanie walked in the opposite direction hand in hand. And when they were out of sight, I peeled open the resealable zipper and tossed the little oat rings into the water. I watched the geese and goslings feed, taking simple delight in their little down faces dipping in and out of the water.

When there was no cereal left, my thoughts turned dark.

Sorrow overcame me.

I was blunted by loss.

And felt so much shame.

For a fleeting second, I wondered how many pills of Xanax were left in the bottle in my handbag.

And how deep the water was.

Mineola

Wednesday, July 5

The subpoena directed me to appear at nine o'clock a.m. in Grand Jury Room 356—and to bring any and all documents contained in the clinical records of Lucas R. Ferro to the proceedings.

I managed to find a parking space in the tiny lot and slipped four hours of quarters in the meter. It was a hot summer morning, so I walked slowly through the hedge-lined pathway to County Criminal Court Building.

As I neared the main entrance, I thought about what I read in the morning newspaper about Luke—that he'd been the target of several brawls at the Nassau County Correctional Center in East Meadow. How he was placed into a more restrictive setting for his own safety. Luke would be alone for twenty-three hours of the day, only having one hour out of the cell to shower, eat, or make calls.

I thought about AJ's parents, Mr. and Mrs. Sheridan, and how broken they were by the murder of their daughter. As I opened the heavy glass entry doors, I wondered if their addiction recovery worsened or improved with this unbearable loss.

Stepping into the building, I brushed my hair to the side and squared the collar of my cotton shirt. I took in a deep breath as I tried to push away everything I felt inside.

The lobby entrance was full of activity with court officers waving scanners around, people moving through metal detectors. Past the check-in area I saw lawyers conferring with clients, families huddling together, photographers checking their cameras, and reporters taking notes. Down the far end of the lobby, broad-shouldered security guards insisted on quiet as people neared the courtroom doors.

I was grateful no one recognized me. I quietly made my way through the metal detector and to the elevators that took me to the building's third floor. A sign indicated Room 356 was at the far end of the East wing of the building. As I reached it, the door was open, and the space was unoccupied.

It was a rather non-descript area, beige-painted walls with similarly colored tiled flooring, a dozen or so mismatched metal chairs, and a small table tucked in the corner. As I stood by the archway of the room, I double-checked the number on the door.

"You're in the right place," a voice called out.

I turned to find a thin young man approaching me. He was dressed in a well-cut blue suit, a white shirt, and a neatly knotted silk tie.

"I'm Assistant District Attorney Jeremy Clark. You must be Dr. Reese."

"Yes, Alicia Reese." I reached out to shake his hand.

"No need to be nervous, Dr. Reese. I'll walk you through it all," he said, escorting me into the room. "This is the grand jury waiting room. The official proceedings take place across the hall, where we'll go in a little while."

He pulled two chairs close together and gestured for me to join him.

"You brought the files we requested?" he asked.

"Yes, I have them right here." I tapped my briefcase with my fingertips.

"Great, may I see them?"

"Of course."

Clark took out a pad and a pen from his chest pocket and jotted some notes as he looked over the file. He had such a youthful face, but as I lingered longer on him, I saw the beginning flecks of gray peek through his jet-black hair, and soft wrinkles surrounded his equally dark eyes. I smelled the faint scent of cigarettes and coffee on his breath as he spoke again.

"Okay. Here's the deal. The Grand Jury room is about as large as this one. There are twenty-three jurors, sitting in chairs just like these, a court reporter and court officer and myself. No judge. No defense attorney. And in case you were worried, no defendant either. You'll sit in the witness bench, which is nothing more than a chair with some window dressing around it. I'll be asking you questions about what happened that night with Ferro. And here's the important part—don't look at me when you answer questions. I want you to look directly at the jurors when giving your testimony, okay?"

I nodded my head. I noticed it felt far too heavy on my neck and shoulders.

"Great. After I ask you my questions, the jurors may have some of their own. Or they may not have any at all. You can never tell, but I want you to be prepared." Clark rose from his seat. "Okay, Dr. Reese. Stay here. I'll be back to get you, but first I have to get things started inside."

Clark placed Luke's file under his arm and left the room.

I slouched back in the chair. Closing my eyes, I thought about Ryan and how I'd rest my hand just beneath his breastbone when we were in his hospice bed. How I'd touch that chakra point, hoping my love flowed through him to strengthen his failing body. Now, at this moment, I opened my eyes, rubbed my hands together, and placed them on my solar plexus.

I heard footsteps echoing in the hall, their sound coming closer and closer to me. I stood up, ready for Clark and met him by the doorway.

"No worries, now, okay?" he said, encouraging me as we walked.

"No worries," I repeated.

Clark opened the jury room door, and a court officer escorted me to the witness bench. As she walked with me, I noticed her right hand held the gun resting in her side holster.

I sat down and looked around the room. Everything was just as Clark described. I made eye contact with the jurors and counted them. Twenty-three. Eleven men and twelve women. Some smiled at me, while others looked down, taking notes. Each had files and papers stacked in front of them.

The room remained quiet as we waited for Clark to close the door and take his seat behind the prosecutorial bench. By his side was an older man, the court reporter, readying his fingers above the stenography machine.

The court officer waited for me to settle into the witness chair and then moved to the side. Within seconds, a stocky court clerk walked in front of me. Next to his official shield, I saw a photo identification badge showing his last name in capital letters, *KEEL*.

"Do you swear to tell the truth, the whole truth and nothing but the truth so help you God?" Keel asked.

I raised my right arm up. "Yes."

"State your name for the record," Clark said from his seat.

"Alicia Reese."

"What is your profession?"

"I'm a psychologist."

"A Ph.D. psychologist, a doctor, correct?

"Yes," I said, nodding to the jurors.

"Please tell the jury what a psychologist does."

"Well, a psychologist is a person who's been trained to do clinical therapy, perform psychological tests, or conduct research. A psychologist can teach at a university setting or do consulting in the business field."

"Just for clarification purposes, a psychologist is different than a psychiatrist, yes?"

"Yes. A psychiatrist is trained as a medical doctor and receives specialized training after medical school in aspects of the mind and behavior, whereas a psychologist is entirely trained in the mind, behavior, and personality, without the medical training."

"Could you go into the differences a bit more, Dr. Reese?"

"There are similarities between psychologists and psychiatrists, so their professions often get confused. But there are differences as well."

I noticed how talking about this clinical aspect helped to alleviate my anxiety. I was never surprised at how my clinical posture centered me.

"Both clinical psychologists and psychiatrists perform psychotherapy. Both are trained in diagnosis and treatment of disorders. But psychiatrists can prescribe medication. For the most part, psychologists do not prescribe."

"So it would be accurate to say that as a psychologist, you provide talk therapy to individuals who seek you out."

"Yes."

"And how long have you been a practicing psychologist?"

"Fifteen years."

"Have you, pursuant to the subpoena, Dr. Reese, brought the records requested to court today?"

"I have."

"And please provide the grand jury the name of the individual who is the subject of those clinical records?"

"Lucas Ferro."

"How do you know Mr. Ferro, Doctor?"

"He was a patient."

"Tell us in what capacity you were treating Mr. Ferro."

"I began working with Mr. Ferro a few weeks ago. He was experiencing panic and anxiety."

"To be specific, you began treating Mr. Ferro on Monday, June 5th 2017, is that correct?"

"Yes, that was the first session."

"And how was treatment progressing?"

"Mr. Ferro had violent urges and was having panic attacks as a result. He was working hard to reduce symptoms and behaviors."

"Doesn't the treatment plan include a provision that Mr. Ferro would call you if his urges were hard to control?"

"Yes, sir."

"In the early morning of Friday, June 23rd, Mr. Ferro called you on your cell at 11:41 p.m. and said he was having a violent impulse."

"Uh –yes."

"Mr. Ferro indicated he had abducted a woman and that he was going to harm her. Is that correct?"

"That's correct."

"So, at the time of the call, Aurora Jean Sheridan was still alive?"

"Yes." A burst of sweat trickled down my neck as I spoke the lie aloud.

"Tell the jury what happened next."

"I told Mr. Ferro I'd be right there."

"Then you called the police"

"I called 911 as soon as I finished speaking with Mr. Ferro. I told the dispatcher where he was and that the police should go there."

"Why did you do that, Dr. Reese?"

"By law, I have to inform the police if a patient communicates a wish, plan, or intent to harm someone."

The room fell quiet. I watched as all the jurors took notes, and then I turned my gaze to where Clark was sitting.

"Thank you, Dr. Reese." Clark turned his attention to the jurors. "Does anyone have any questions before we dismiss this witness?"

I felt a wave of panic as Clark asked the jurors. I took in a deep breath and exhaled slowly. I worried if I could stay composed if more detailed questions were asked.

I looked at them.

Shrugs, nods, and silence.

No one appeared eager to ask any questions.

"Let the record reflect, no questions from the grand jury for this witness," Clark said. "Dr. Reese, you can go now. The court thanks you for your time."

I said nothing but nodded. I looked at Clark as I exited the witness bench and smiled thinly to the jurors as the court officer Keel escorted me to the door.

As it closed behind me, an enormous wave of panic hit. I hurried down the hallway to the elevator, fighting the sudden hyperventilation.

Changing my mind, I took the stairs instead and pushed through the choking sensations as I ran down the steps. My chest tightened as I passed several people in the staircase, and my legs began to feel weak as I neared the lobby. A dizzying haze gripped me as I exited the building and made my way to the car. But I couldn't outrun the mounting anxiety, and I let it take hold of me as I slumped in the driver's seat.

It was a long while before I was able to leave the parking lot.

I knew that the Grand Jury itself didn't determine a person's guilt or innocence. The Grand Jury only determined whether there was enough evidence to indict a person. In New York State, there'd have to be at least twelve votes to register an indictment in a criminal case.

When I called in for my messages later that afternoon, there was a one from Clark.

"Hi Dr. Reese. It's Jeremy Clark. Wanted to thank you for today—and to let you know the Grand Jury made a unanimous decision. Ferro will be charged with one count of intentional murder, murder in the second degree, and one count of rape in the first degree. If Ferro goes to trial and is found guilty, he'd likely serve two consecutive 25 year to life sentences. I'll let you know when the case gets calendared—for days we're going to need you to testify. But that's not going to be for a while, though. Okay, I'll be in touch."

I listened to the message again.

I replayed it three more times.

And then deleted it.

Oyster Bay

Friday, July 14

I stayed in bed until early afternoon. I didn't have to be in the office until two o'clock, but I did have to get moving.

I'd spent the last two weeks dodging the media as the Associated Press picked up the Sheridan murder from the news wires. What began as a local story was now a national headline. The twenty-four hour cable news stations obsessed over the case, inviting legal and psychological pundits to mull over the specifics of the Tarasoff ruling in hotly debated formats.

Morning television programs joined sensationalism with segments like *"Therapy and Confidentiality—What You Need to Know."* Newspapers featured pictures of Luke, AJ, and the ongoing investigation.

Photographers took pictures and videos of me walking by my home, walking into my office, and driving in my car. I felt the knowing stares from strangers when I made the necessary trips out of my house. Shopping. Gassing up the car.

Living with the decision I chose wasn't easy. Not that I thought it would be. But I didn't anticipate how living with a lie would press so heavily on me.

Some moments, I considered my abandonment of professional ethics the right thing and a brave decision. Luke was a psychopath. Recovery for him was poor. But my betrayal was a duplicitous act.

I found I was suffering physically with splintering headaches and back pain. I wasn't sleeping well, and when I did, I found myself recalling disturbing dreams the next morning. I worried if I couldn't find a better way to cope with this conflict, an emotional and physical collapse would soon follow.

The decision to stop practicing grew within me during this time. I couldn't continue to do clinical work because I crossed the ethical line. Making that decision helped me atone for my transgression with Luke. It also put to rest the conflicts Dr. Prader had about my future professional life.

I took a long shower, letting the mist of the hot water surround me. I lingered in the steam, allowing the warmth to awaken, comfort, and revive me. The lavender body wash helped to lift my mood, and before long, I felt myself emerging into the here and now.

I dressed, dried my hair, and put on a touch of makeup. I didn't have much of an appetite, but I grabbed an energy bar from the cupboard and nibbled at it as I drove to the office.

"Thanks for meeting me here, Pete," I said.

"How are things, Doc?"

"Pretty good, all things considered."

"When did you want to leave the building?"

"Well, the lease is up in eight months. Is there any way we can make that happen sooner?"

Peter Carruthers was a successful real estate entrepreneur with many office properties on the North Shore of Nassau County. He was an older man, glossy though not slick, but a businessman nonetheless. I didn't know what to expect about breaking the lease.

"To tell you the truth, I hate seeing my building in the paper and on the television. Not good for business."

"I bet."

"You've been with me a long time. Never late with a payment, even when things were bad for you."

"So what are you thinking, Pete?"

"I'm thinking, give me one more month's rent, and we'll call it a day."

"That's generous."

"I'll get the papers drawn and have them sent to you ASAP." Pete reached out and grabbed my hand tightly, giving it a squeeze. "Listen, kid, you need to find some good luck out there."

"Yeah, I know."

I reached forward and hugged Peter, which took him by surprise, given our relationship was quite a formal one. Then I turned and proceeded down to my office, not giving him a chance to say anything else.

I spent the rest of the day calling patients and setting up appointments in order to terminate my work with them. The recent events made it easy for them—as well as my colleagues—to understand my need to stop working.

The important task though, was not to make this about me, but to make this unplanned transition for my patients to new therapists as easy as possible. So many emotions regarding my departure would arise, and I wanted every patient to have time to process them with me.

I pulled a heavy tufted chair up to the long picture window. I lifted the blinds as far as the cord would take them, filling the room with a magnificent glow of light. I sat down, leaned my elbows on the cool window frame, and rested my chin on my hands.

The beach was busy with people sunning themselves. Children were digging in the sand, running by the water's edge. On the bay, several jet skis zoomed across the water, careful not to interrupt a nearby motorboat and its water skier.

In the distance, I saw the sails of long-necked boats finding the wind, while others set anchor in well-chosen spots.

And across the bay, on Centre Island, my eyes took in each of the mansions that graced the coastline.

I loved this view.

I loved this place.

And I loved my work.

Those sentiments were, clearly and forever, in the past tense now.

I lifted my hands up, palms towards me, and then pivoted them away in a turning motion. It's the sign for *finished.* It's the sign for *all done.*

That's what I felt.

And that's all it was.

Mineola

Tuesday, July 18

D etective Skolnik asked me to come to the Homicide Squad first thing in the morning, so I arrived promptly at nine a.m.

I parked my car on Franklin Avenue and took the sidewalk path to the Nassau County Police Headquarters. Before I reached the entry doors, I passed the Police Memorial Park, which honored officers who died in the line of duty. I noticed the half-mast flags sloped downward, stock-still from the windless summer heat of the day.

I entered the building and checked the directory for the Homicide Division. I walked up one flight of stairs and tried to keep my nervousness under wraps.

"Deep blue ocean water," I said, using imagery to relax. I paused before entering the squad room. "Cool green cut grass."

I swung the door open to find the room bustling with activity. In an alcove apart from the squad room, I saw a tiny waiting area.

"Dr. Reese to see Detective Skolnik," I said to the woman typing at a desk.

"He expecting you?"

"Yes."

She stopped her fingers mid-air and whisked off her bifocals to get a good look at me. She jogged her head to the side. "In there."

I moved into the center of the squad room and looked for Detective Skolnik. I found him near the coffee maker.

"Detective?"

"Yeah?" Skolnik said, looking confused. "Oh, Dr. Reese."

144

"You did say first thing this morning, right?"

"Yeah. I did. Forgot what you looked like." Skolnik walked to his desk and motioned for me to follow, dragging a chair for me to sit in.

"So, what questions do you want to ask me?"

"Just a couple of things. Shouldn't take too long,"

"Will Detective Lombardi be joining us?" I asked, preferring her good cop persona over his bad cop one.

"She should be here soon." Skolnik pulled out Luke's file and thrust his thick index finger to a spot on the paper. "You were working with Ferro only a month, right?"

"Just over three weeks."

"Ever met him before that?"

"No."

"So, he makes an appointment, you work with him a while, and then he murders the Sheridan girl."

"Uh, yeah."

"And you never saw him before that."

"Right."

Skolnik scribbled some notes and shook his head in a slow and deliberate manner.

"Why are you asking me this?"

"No need to get uptight, Doc," Skolnik said.

"We're just checking logistics," Lombardi said, pulling a chair up. "Did you know Ferro beyond your working relationship?"

"You mean, outside of the office?"

"Yes. Did you have a personal relationship with the suspect?" Lombardi asked.

"No. Why would you think that?"

"So, there'd be no reason for him to be seeing you outside of the sessions," Lombardi said.

"Yes. No reason."

My anxiety began to worsen. Agitated, I looked at Lombardi and Skolnik, trying to figure out what they were trying to get at. "Is this about the black Cadillac?" I asked suddenly.

"What Cadillac?" Lombardi asked.

"I called and left a message with a Detective after Luke was arrested. Detective Silvestri. He said you weren't in and that I could leave the information with him."

"Doc, there's no Silvestri in homicide," Lombardi said.

"Jesus Christ, she means Sal Vestrese," Skolnik said, slamming his fist on the table. "Goddamn clerk never takes a good message." Skolnik stretched out his neck, jutted his jaw, and tried to compose himself. "What did you tell Vestrese?"

"I thought you should know that for a while, I noticed this black car around my house a couple of times. At first, I thought it could be Luke. I was able to get the first three letters of the license plate and had a friend run a check for me."

"What did you find out?" Skolnik asked.

"Car's part of a fleet of limousines. They do business somewhere in Manhattan, I think." I opened a zipped partition in my handbag and pulled out the sheet Steve gave me a while back.

Skolnik looked at Lombardi. "I'll run it."

"Listen, that's not what we're talking about," Lombardi continued. "We found some photos at Ferro's place."

"Photos? Of what?"

"He was in your house, Doc," Lombardi said. "Several times."

I watched her pull out a pile of pictures from Ferro's file. Each was enclosed in a plastic bag and sealed with a bright red evidence label. She placed one photo after another in front of me.

"He was obviously stalking you," she said.

I couldn't take it in the first time. My eyes darted from one image to another. The insides of my stomach railed up hard against my spine. Soon, foamy white blotches of light swirled in circles, but no matter how hard I tried, they clouded my vision. I fought the choking panic but lost the battle. I stumbled to a nearby trashcan and vomited.

As the episode passed, I realized the squad room was utterly silent. I skimmed the back of my hand across my mouth and fought the heaving that rippled upwards again.

"Let's go." Detective Lombardi pulled me out of the room.

"Oh, god," I said, trying to walk.

Lombardi turned the doorknob to the women's bathroom and held the door open for me with her strong body. She caught my eye. "Take your time."

As the door clicked shut, I moved to the sink and twisted the faucet. I swirled several handfuls of water in my mouth, spitting away the wretched bits that remained.

Though I was pale and sweaty, I did my best to collect myself. I patted my face dry with a paper towel and smoothed my clothing back in place—and the messy pieces of my hair, combing them with my fingers.

A horror crept into the hollow of my stomach as I thought of him in my home, in my room, in my space. I shut my eyes to stop the stirring visions.

I turned away from the mirror and paced the floor. My clinical skills were emerging, which gave me the momentum I needed.

Was the stalking predatory?

Was it intimacy seeking?

I realized I'd never have the opportunity to explore any of these things with Luke. Looking at the photos again, though, would give me some insight.

"I'm ready," I said to Lombardi as I exited the bathroom.

"We can do this another time, Doc," she said.

"No. Let's finish it."

It was business as usual when we returned to the squad room, as if what happened moments ago was a daily humdrum occurrence. People were re-engaged in their activities, the floor was cleaned, and a new trashcan rested next to Skolnik's desk.

"Here," Skolnik said, flexing his arm out as I sat down. The peppermint candy looked so small resting in his broad hand. "Show's over, right?"

"Tank's empty," Lombardi said with a smile.

I unwrapped the plastic casing and popped it in my mouth. "Thanks," I said, grateful to taste something sweet.

"We found these in Ferro's house—under the floorboards in his bedroom," Lombardi said, returning to the photos. "We think he was in your house a few times."

"While I was sleeping," I said, holding several of the pictures in my hands.

Skolnik and Lombardi remained quiet and watched my every move.

"He was standing right over me," I continued, stunned and bewildered.

"I know this must be hard," Lombardi said.

Luke was there at least three times, given the different clothes in the pictures. He took photos of each room in the house, and there were several images of Elvis sleeping. I felt a cold numbness sink in my body as I looked at them again.

"Your house alarmed?" Skolnik asked.

"Yes. Every window and every door," I said. For a moment, I looked upward toward the ceiling and remembered the few times Elvis got out from the loft window. "Shit, I think he came in through the one window I have on the second floor."

"It ain't wired?" Skolnik asked.

"It's such a high window, we never bothered rigging it."

"Gotta get crime scene there," Skolnik said to Lombardi.

"There's more, Doc," Lombardi said. "We need to know where these were taken?"

I clutched my stomach as a dozen more pictures came out. "I don't know what this is. It's not my house." I said.

"You don't recognize anything here?" Skolnik asked.

"No."

"What about these?" Lombardi asked, setting down more photographs as Skolnik gathered the others.

"This is my sister, Nicole. Her husband, Keith. My niece and nephew." I clenched my teeth. "God dammit, he was there—at their house too?" It took a second, but I grabbed Skolnik by the arm. "Let me see those other pictures again."

Detective Skolnik fanned them out again in front of me.

"These are from the break-in next door to my sister. This happened a few weeks ago. Call Detective Randy Scott in the second precinct."

"Why would Ferro break-in to the neighbor's?" Skolnik asked Lombardi.

"Because he thought it was Nicole's house. The numbers in the court aren't sequential. Even the mail gets mixed up there," I said. "Soraya Rahm is 4, my sister is 4A. Easy to get it wrong."

"We got more, Doc. What about these?" Lombardo asked.

"This one's the hospital. I go to supervision there once a week with Dr. Susan Prader," I said, shifting through the pictures. "Christ, he took a photo of his case file that she keeps."

"And this one?" Skolnik asked.

"Oh my god. Seth. My nephew." I swallowed hard, recalling that moment. The clothes on the floor, the Mets jacket on the bed. I could see Seth in the picture and a reflection of Luke holding a camera up in the mirror by the closet. "This is the loft in my house."

"Did your nephew mention meeting Ferro?" Lombardi asked.

"He said Ryan, my husband, was talking to him in the loft. My sister and I thought it was just a grief reaction."

"Ferro kinda resembles your late husband, doesn't he?" Lombardi asked.

I widened my eyes. "No, he doesn't."

"Dark hair, blue eyes, muscular build. And with that Mets shirt on, I can see how your nephew could mistake him for your husband. Especially, if the kid's in a messed up state of mind," Lombardi continued.

I studied the photo. And there was a likeness—slight enough to see now.

Is this the real reason I wanted to work with Luke? That he reminded me of Ryan? I asked myself. *Am I that out of touch with my subconscious?*

Lombardi took the photo from my hand, halting my inner thoughts.

"How do you know what my husband looks like?" I asked, feeling embarrassed and exposed.

"We know everything there is to know about you, Dr. Reese. It's what we do here," Skolnik said.

"Listen, I know this is a lot to take in," Lombardi cut in, wrapping things up. "If you think of anything else, let us know."

"So, that's it?" I asked.

"For now, yeah," Skolnik said.

"We'll be in touch," Lombardi said, collecting the rest of the photos. She made a quick exit away from the desk and out of the room.

Skolnik was slower and slid his chair out from under him with a pokey thrust. "You're lucky," he said. "He was after you too."

"Yes, lucky," I said as I got up and left.

East Meadow

Wednesday, July 19

The Nassau County Correctional Center in East Meadow was a maximum-security facility, where nearly two thousand inmates awaited trial, sentencing, or served time. I drove through the security gate, and I wondered if Luke would even come out to see me.

"Who you here to see?" a correction officer asked.

"Lucas Ferro."

"He expecting you?"

"No, he's not."

"Gonna take a while. Sign in here and go to the visitor's lounge. We'll call you."

I walked up to the metal detector, placed my keys and my handbag on the conveyor belt, and watched them roll to the other side. I passed through the detector's frame without any problems.

As I walked to the lounge, I pulled out a piece of gum from my pocket, chewing hard until it was soft in my mouth. I took a seat facing the inmate doorway at an empty table that was small and circular. It reminded me of the tables in my elementary school, where students worked together doing group projects.

While I waited, I thought about the pictures Skolnik and Lombardi showed me. After the shock of it all, I was able to see something in the images that was profoundly symbolic.

I recalled how Luke said he never truly liked being alone. How he wished for comfort as a child and spoke about never having it. There was no denying the disturbing aspects of Luke's behavior. I was enraged and felt violated, but I also realized how his pathology pushed him to such limits.

I imagined the pictures again through a clinical lens—subtracting terror from the equation. The first images I saw were peaceful and even pleasant. Elvis was tucked in his bed or was resting beside his cat toys. Me sleeping. Even the ones of the house—a tea kettle in the kitchen. The velvet blanket draped on the sofa. The basket of soaps in the bathroom. The teddy bear on the rocking chair in the loft.

But the ones of Nicole, Keith, and the kids seemed less about comfort and more about family. The twins playing on the swings. Keith and Nicole embracing in the pool.

The one of Seth in the loft with Luke was hardest to for me to think about clinically. I was furious how Luke's lack of boundaries upset Seth. And then I wondered if Dr. Prader was in danger knowing about all Luke did. Would he have hurt her too?

A loud clanging of metal doors brought me back to the present. I saw Luke come into the visitor's lounge with a corrections officer beside him. I watched as he looked in from the doorway—scanning each table, then moving to the next one to find who was waiting for him.

I waited for his eyes to catch mine. He hesitated a moment, and for a second, I thought he'd turn back. But he walked to where I was sitting with the corrections officer following behind.

Luke was dressed in a loose fitting orange jumpsuit and a pair of white colored sneakers, the kind that slide on. His face was thin, and several days of stubble budded into a patchy beard. When he lifted his hands and placed them on the table, I noticed that his knuckles were scabbed over.

"You got some fucking nerve," he began, talking tightly through a forced smile. "I should fucking kill you right here."

"You were supposed to call me. That was the plan. And don't tell me how fast the urge came because that's bullshit."

He glared at me and then took his gaze to the floor. As he did, I looked over to the corrections officer who was now leaning against the wall.

"So you just hang me out to dry? Could've just walked away. Not treat me anymore."

He was right and I had no response. Instead, I leaned closer to him. "I want some answers, Luke."

"You wanna play 21 questions?"

"Look around. This isn't a game," I said.

"Well, this ain't therapy either."

"Certainly is not," I replied.

Ferro pulled his face tight, scowling right at me and fell silent.

"Cops said you crossed paths with AJ in the mall. But really, how'd you meet?" I asked him.

"Found her smoking a cigarette on the curb one night when I was passing by your house."

"Passing by?" I snapped back. "You *broke* into my house."

"Cops showed you those pictures, huh?" Luke said, surprised.

"Why? Why my family? My supervisor? Why the hell were you in my home? Touching my things . . . there when I was asleep?"

"You were learning everything about me." Luke paused. "Thought it was only fair I did the same."

I narrowed my eyes and reflected on his answer. *There's more to this*, I thought to myself.

Before I could press further, Luke changed the subject.

"AJ liked my car. *Red like my hair*, she said to me. We flirted. Made plans to hook up," he said. "Was having a good time for a few weeks till you came along—busting up her ankle."

"And you were there, flashing the high beams. Hauling ass so I wouldn't recognize your car," I said.

Luke raised his brows. "You knew?"

"Not that night," I said as my eyes brimmed. "I wish I did. She'd be alive now because I would've stopped working with you right then."

"She wasn't long for this world anyway," Luke said. "She wasn't a nice girl, Dr. Reese."

Clenching my jaw and blinking back tears, I shoved my face right up to his.

"I bet you're right. I bet AJ *wasn't* a nice girl. She saw through you. Quick and fast. She got bored or worse—wanted to ditch you. And when you couldn't get what you wanted from her anymore, you got violent. And she fought back. Not like some naïve, nice girl. I bet she was fierce. And arrogant. And that pissed you off. Poor little boy."

"Very unprofessional, Doc. But nice try," Luke replied.

I leaned back, trying to gain my composure. But I couldn't keep my feelings in check. I was so raw and hurt.

"Did you rape her and then kill her? Or kill her first? I understand that's a big deal when you're in here. The timeline and all."

I widened my eyes and looked around towards the other inmates sitting nearby.

Luke didn't flinch.

"Sounds like you may be a little jealous, Doc. We did have a good thing going, you and me. You're the one who fucked all that up. But listen, you don't have to worry about me. Really, Doc, you should be worrying about yourself," he said.

"Why's that?"

"Because when we go to trial, I'm gonna ruin you."

"This case *isn't* going to trial, and you're *not* going to ruin me."

"Really?"

"Yes. And here's why." I sat back, catching my breath. "You've seen me violate privilege. And I won't hesitate to violate it again. To protect myself— or anyone—from you. And next time, the police won't know where the information came from. So if you want to keep yourself from the execution chamber in Florida...you remember Florida, right? Then you'll plead this case out."

"You fucking bitch," he yelled, finally boiling over with rage.

Luke jumped the table and sliced my lip open with a rock-hard punch to the mouth. He grabbed me as I fell to the floor and readied his fist for another swing. In seconds, the corrections officer stopped Luke, yanking back his arm—while another officer rushed forward with his baton, pressing it hard against Luke's chest.

"You okay, Ma'am?" another officer asked, helping me up from the floor.

"Yeah."

"This isn't finished," Luke said, pitching his weight against the guards.

As the officer moved me away from the commotion, a dull realization swelled, followed by a flashback of the photos Skolnik and Lombardi showed me. My mind raced and then suddenly seized on the pictures of Nicole, Keith, and the twins.

And Shasta.

"You drugged the dog!" I shouted as they dragged Luke out an emergency exit.

His eyes narrowed. Then his mouth curled into a tight-lipped, self-satisfied grin just as the doors locked shut.

My heart, pounding with fury and terror, slowed as the officer took me out of the visiting area.

"He drugged Shasta," I muttered to him.

"I heard," he replied, guiding me to a nearby chair.

The officer waited by my side as I leaned back and slowed my breathing. While I calmed down, I remembered how I came here to find answers. And to draw a line in the sand. I realized what a fearless move it was as I grabbed a tissue from my pocket and wiped away the blood from my chin.

"Thanks. I'm good now," I said after a few moments.

Just before he walked away, he pointed to my mouth. "Better ice that."

I nodded, feeling the swollen parts of my face with my fingertips.

When I made my way out of the prison, I couldn't decide which way to drive home. I could go East on Hempstead Turnpike and then up Jerusalem Avenue back home. Or take the Seaford Oyster Bay Expressway northbound.

Or drive the side streets, winding my way back the long way to Brookville.

I went west.

Boulder

Saturday, August 19th

"These are all the original hardwood floors, but the kitchen and baths were remodeled about two years ago," Toni from Millennium Homes told me.

"Nice," I said.

"You can see all the appliances are top line. Look at these French doors. Gorgeous, right? And upstairs you have two bedrooms and plenty of closet space."

"What did you say about the garage?" I asked.

"It's heated. Great feature to have here in winter. And did I tell you there's a flagstone patio and a hot tub?"

"Yes, and the mountain views are just as beautiful as you described."

"It's less than three miles from the university," she said, looking at my application form. "And the local shopping is great here."

The house was contemporary in architecture, with angled walls, vaulted gables, and large modern windows. I liked what I saw, but the need to satisfy my guilt was never too far away. I bit the cuticle of my thumb, causing it to bleed again.

When Ryan died, I mourned for him. Like many people who lose someone they love, I had to learn how to grieve but also how to take care of my own needs. And like so many people, I often felt a sense of survivor's guilt—why was he the one who got ill? Why was I spared? Over time, I was able to navigate my way through the rough waters and moved through the stages of bereavement as expected. I was able to invite moments of happiness in without the need to quickly push them away.

But the experience with Luke distorted my world. The choices I made re-activated my levels of guilt and grief—and added self-blame to the mix.

"This is the first floor bedroom. The current owners used it as an office," Toni continued.

"This leads outside?" I asked, heading to a sliding glass door.

"Yes. See? The lock is right here." She showed it to me as though it was mine.

I stepped out from the bedroom onto the massive rectangular patio. The Colorado air was smooth and dry, and the mountains in the distance were a colorful mix of sienna, purple, and green. The clouds floated above, feathery and light, layer upon layer upon layer.

I'd miss the amniotic feel of Oyster Bay, but it was beautiful here in Colorado in its own way. The house was bigger than I needed, more than I wanted to spend, but there was something healing about it from the moment I saw it.

"What's the rent again?"

"Two thousand a month."

"I'll take it."

"I'll call the office and get the papers drawn up."

"Great. I'll have a look around while you do that."

My transition to Colorado was going well. I arrived a week ago, taking up residence at a local hotel in University Village. The faculty position I accepted at the University of Colorado involved teaching psychoanalytic theory and personality testing—something I knew well. The psychology department welcomed me warmly, as did the students. Within days, I settled into my small, yet practical office on campus.

I left the practice of psychotherapy behind with the knowledge I'd never go back to it. I had no intention of taking the licensing exam in Colorado, and I'd eventually let my New York license lapse. University life was a way for me to still be part of the field I loved. My passion for psychology and keen diagnostic ability would be harnessed for teaching students, not for treating patients. My clinical experience and analytic training would highlight lesson plans, not treatment plans. All in all, it was a good fit.

I applied for the teaching position a few days after seeing Luke in jail. And when the job was offered, I put my Brookville house on the market.

Though I grew up and lived on Long Island my entire life, it was no longer a place for me to be. Losing Ryan was hard enough, but what was set into motion with Luke made life even more traumatic. I couldn't escape the cutting edges of my transgression, but, with distance, maybe I could manage the crushing burden of it.

My decision to move was hard for Nicole, but she and Keith, and the few friends I had, thought the change might be good for me. The toll of the Sheridan murder was visible to anyone who knew me. Even Dr. Prader supported going to Colorado.

Turning my attention back to the house, I looked at the mountain range of the Flatiron foothills from one of the windows, taking in its striking rustic landscape and thought of Ryan. He visited Colorado as a teenager and always wanted to take me there—to see a concert at the Red Rocks Amphitheatre, whitewater raft down the Colorado River. During one of our last conversations, he made me promise I'd come here someday. I told him I would, helping him pass with a sense of closure. It felt fitting to be here.

"Dr. Reese," Toni called from the bottom of the stairs.

"Yes?"

"I'm gonna head over to the office and get the lease ready. Why don't you meet me there in a little while?"

I walked down the stairs. "Great idea." I smiled and shook her hand. "Thanks so much."

"You're going to love it here."

I strolled along the property, which was lined with colorful wildflowers, white yarrow and fringed sage, rugged shrubs, and sturdy trees. From the backyard, I saw the grandeur of the mountains again.

Gazing skyward, I wondered about Luke. He was always on the edge of my mind, and the custom of contrasting my life with his was a common occurrence. The reality of what happened was always with me, and I didn't expect the experience to fade with time. The phenomenon of rage and ruin would forever bind us together.

I toed a nearby rock and felt a wave of sorrow wrench within me. I remained quiet for a while and thought about the past few months of my life and the changes that continued to occur. The contradiction that I had become.

I sat down on the edge of the patio and set my handbag near my side. I reached for my wallet. In one of the accordion style compartments were two neatly folded faxes ADA Clark sent to me the day before. One was a short section of the court proceedings. The other was a letter saying that my testimony at the turn of the New Year would *not* be necessary because a plea deal was arranged with the DA's office and Luke's Defense Attorney, Lauren Kubrick.

"It was an unlikely turn of events," Clark wrote, "and one that certainly serves justice."

The court proceedings read as follows:

> On August 22, 2017, The Honorable Judge Jonathan Greene of the Criminal Court of Nassau County rendered his sentence of defendant, Lucas R. Ferro, for the charge of intentional murder—murder in the second degree, which is a class A-I felony, in violation of New York Penal Law §125.25, and for a count of rape in the first degree, a class B felony in violation of New York Penal code §130.35. As arranged in the plea agreement, Lucas R. Ferro would serve a concurrent sentence of 25 years to life in jail.

The plea arrangement offered concurrent sentences—a perk for not wasting the county's court time and money. And with that comes a chance that he'd have some kind of life. If Luke served his time, without incident, he'd be in his fifties when he got out. It was a smart decision.

I had no plan to further betray Luke, though. He couldn't harm anyone anymore.

No more murder.

No more death.

It was an ending to all of that.

Syosset

Wednesday, January 3

A s soon as the fall semester ended at the university, I flew to New York to spend Christmas and New Year's with Nicole, Keith, and the twins. I also arranged for the closing of the Brookville house to happen at that time—making it easy for me to tie up all those loose ends.

I arrived at New York's LaGuardia airport, taking the red-eye in from Colorado and rented a minivan to get around town. I needed a roomy vehicle to lug all the things I left in the house. Pictures. Clothes. Precious trinkets. A moving company would ship the big pieces of furniture. Then there was my library of psychology books. Which ones to keep. Which ones to give away to colleagues.

In the time that passed while I was in Colorado, the newsworthiness of AJ's murder faded. I no longer felt nervous being in New York.

I was yesterday's news. Of no interest to anyone but my family and a few friends.

And it was easy for me to fade away, becoming secluded in my own world in Colorado. I slipped into the quiet isolation of life there just as I did living as a Coda in the hearing world or in the Deaf world.

The house closing was scheduled for today, so a lot was happening. The movers were coming at noon, the buyers would arrive for a final walk-through around 2:00 p.m., and the closing was at 3:30 p.m. After the closing, I'd have dinner at Nicole's and spend the rest of the week there before going back to Boulder.

A stop at Mae's Bakery for a much needed coffee and pastry was first on my morning agenda. Then I'd go to the UPS Store. Before I left New York, I rented a large post office box to get the mail that didn't make its way to me in Colorado.

I pulled into a parking space on Jackson Avenue near the bakery and noticed that nothing had changed in the three months since I had left. Except for the weather. The warm colors of summer were traded for gray skies and crisp wintry air.

I took the concrete sidewalk to the bakery and pulled the door open. The sweet smells of confections were glorious. I pulled a number from the ticket machine and waited my turn.

"Is that you, Alicia?"

"Sure is, Mae."

"I didn't recognize ya," Mae said, her Irish brogue still as thick as ever.

"Happy New Year." I reached over the glass counter to kiss her. "So good to see you."

"How's Colorado, darlin'?" she asked.

"It's a nice change. I miss New York, though."

"Well, it takes time." From head to toe, Mae looked me over. "Are ya eatin'? Ya wouldn't even make a shadow t'were the sun out."

I wasn't eating. I wasn't sleeping. I was a mess. I felt lost, depressed, and angry. But I'd never acknowledge that to her. Or anyone.

"Oh, I'm fine. Just busy getting settled in." I moved our conversation to the display counter. "Mmmm. These look delicious."

"The raspberry ones?"

"Yes. I'll take one now, and give me three chocolate ones to go. Oh, and a couple of those rainbow sprinkled cookies. I'm heading out to Nic's later."

"She was in a while ago. The kids are growin' like weeds."

"I know. Time flies," I said making myself a cup of coffee.

"Sure does." Mae smiled and turned away to start putting together the order.

Mae's Bakery was in business in Syosset over 50 years. It was well known not just only in town, but on Long Island. Old world traditions. Handcrafted delicacies. Award winning cakes and pastries. I came here as a kid, worked here as a teen, and made it a frequent habit as an adult. I knew Mae my entire life, just as she knew me.

And we both knew I wasn't at my best.

"Twelve-eighty, dear."

"I'll see you again when I come back for Easter—in April."

"Great. I'll expect to see ya then."As she passed me the boxes, she patted my hand. "Take care," she signed, making the letter *k* with her fingers and tapping them on top of one another.

"Same to you," I signed.

I smiled to her through the window as I left and walked back to the minivan. I set the boxes of pastries on the passenger door seat and started toward the UPS Store, which was a few yards away.

I drank my coffee and finished the raspberry croissant along the way. A few times, I caught my reflection in the store windows. Mae was right. I was thin. And it troubled me that I hadn't really noticed.

The door to the UPS Store chimed as I walked in. I singled out the key on my keychain, looked for the post office box, and opened the door.

Peering in, I saw a pile of letters, papers, magazines, and flyers filling the entire space. I reached in and pulled out as much as my hands could hold, but there was more than I realized. I needed something to carry the mail.

I walked to the back of the store and asked the young clerk if he had any unused boxes I could use. Without moving from his seat, he nudged a nearby carton my way with his foot. "Use this," he said.

I walked closer to him, almost behind the register, and picked it up. I didn't thank him or look at him, but I allowed my annoyance to trump his indifference.

I was almost near the minivan when my eye caught a patch of handwriting on an envelope that dipped and shifted in the carton as I walked. I'd seen the handwriting before. It was familiar. I'd seen it before on a check. But it took a second for my mind to make the connection. When I saw the postmark from Ossining Jail in New York, I realized it was from Luke.

My hands trembled as I rushed to the minivan, pressed the key fob, and opened the door. I balanced the carton on the console between the two captain's chairs, plunked myself down in the driver's seat, and slammed the door shut.

I lifted the seal of the envelope with my fingers. I pulled out the lined sheet of yellow paper and opened the neatly creased folds.

> Sometimes the hard thing to do and the right
> thing to do are one and the same. 2.8 miles east.
> 143 steps. Wax Murtle Tree. Perembrooke.

"Perembrooke." I recognized the name, reading it in Luke's newspaper article—and the others that were written in <u>The Miami Free Press</u> newspaper.

Sheriff John Perembrooke was in charge of the Donald Gallin investigation.

He wants me to let Perembrooke know where Gallin is buried.

I read the note again.

Sometimes the hard thing to do and the right thing to do are one and the same.

I remembered saying that to Luke many months ago. It was one of many phrases I used a lot in therapy. It highlighted the complexity of conflict. How choosing to do something right can also be hard. Very hard. But that doing so, leads to redemption.

Luke was clearly reaching out for some kind of emotional deliverance.

I picked up the phone and dialed 711 to make a relay call.

I'd be getting to Huntington later than expected.

Oyster Bay

Thursday, January 4

From Main Street, the office building was quiet except for the lights in the chiropractor's first floor office.

I looked up to where my office used to be. It was dark with the shades drawn.

Security was provided for the office building until dusk. Since night fell fast in October, Steve would be keeping shorter hours at the helm. He was a retired New York City Police Officer and never complained of the hours being too long or too short. He was happy to be working. And whenever Carruther's Realty needed him, he was there.

Now I needed him.

I looked for Steve at the kiosk as I pulled in; it was almost five o'clock. Since he was a man of strict habits, he'd likely be closing the two side entrances and the back doors. Making them secure for the night.

I drove slowly past the right side door and then around to the back. As I turned the second corner of the building, I found him making his security loop in his truck. I slowed the minivan as I approached and flicked my lights. I knew he didn't recognize the car or me behind the wheel as I drove closer. Everything was out of context.

I lowered my passenger window as I pulled up next to him.

"Steve, it's Alicia," I said.

It took him a second, and then he blurted, "Doc!"

"Got a minute for me? I need your help."

"Lemme get to the booth, and we can talk there," he said, and drove off toward the office lot entryway.

I followed and parked alongside his security truck.

Steve waited for me to get out, and together, we walked over to the kiosk and stepped onto the platform's ledge.

"What's doing?"

"I need to know how to make a phone call that won't be traced."

Steve was quiet and stared at me hard. "Well, the best way is to buy a burner phone. In cash."

"Okay. Where do I do that?"

"In the city. You can find burners on the street. And I know a few areas where big brother ain't looking."

"Security cameras."

"Right. This way, if you stay on long enough for a trace, your face won't—"

I interrupted him. "Should I use gloves?"

"You could. Or you could just wipe the phone down."

"Good idea."

"Yeah." Steve regarded me seriously. "Tell me you're not in any trouble, Doc."

"I'm not, Steve. But I have to make a call, and it needs to be private."

In the fifteen years that our paths crossed, our connection was always one of affection and regard. He was fatherly in his ways, and I welcomed his interest and concern, as he did mine. But the tone of this exchange was different from any of our conversations. I wasn't sure if Steve wanted to know more before he gave me what I needed.

He walked into the booth and began writing.

"Go here, near The Garden to find a burner—and head to the corner of 1st Avenue and 10th Street for a camera free zone."

"Night is better than day?"

"Always better at night."

"Thanks. I knew I could come to you."

"You need me for anything, you call me. Still got my number, right?"

"I do." I touched his cheek as I turned to leave.

"You goin' there now?" Steve asked, stepping off the platform.

"No rest for the weary."

Steve watched me get in, crank the engine, and pull out of the parking space. As I drove up to the exit, I stuck my head out of the window.

"Stay outta trouble now," I said.

"You know it, Doc."

A moment later, I turned out onto the road and headed for the Long Island Expressway. I took it West all the way into Manhattan.

I turned right on 35th Street and took it cross-town to 7th Avenue, where I found a parking space two blocks from Madison Square Garden. I walked to where Steve said I'd find the guys hawking burner phones, and within minutes, I purchased one for thirty dollars.

I hailed a cab to the corner of 1st Avenue and 9th Street. I strolled slowly up to 10th and found little pub, named Watson's, to make the call. I walked to the back of the bar, into an empty restroom, and slid the lock.

The day before, I bought a top of the line voice scrambler at the local spy store, paying for it in cash. It would change the voice, pitch, and timbre of my own voice. A way for me to stay protected. I put the setting on so that my voice would be a man's voice.

I turned it on and dialed 1-305-555-1212 on the burner phone.

"Welcome to Bellsouth information. What city and listing please?" a computerized voice asked.

"Miami, Florida. Miami-Dade Police Department."

"I'm sorry, what city and listing?"

"Miami. Miami-Dade Police Department," I said. This time louder.

I heard a click and thought I was disconnected.

"What city and listing?" a man asked.

"Miami-Dade Police Department. Florida."

"I have Non-Emergency or Administration Offices?"

"Let's try administration offices."

"Please hold for the number."

"The number is area code 3-0-5-5-5-5-6-6-4-0."

I wrote it down and waited for the cell phone carrier to connect to the number. The phone rang once, then twice. My heart stuck in my throat as it rang again. And then again. Five rings now.

No one's there, I thought to myself. A quick look at my watch showed 8:42 p.m. Then, a click.

"Hello, Miami-Dade Police Department. How can I direct your call?"

"John Perembrooke's voice mail."

I didn't know if Perembrooke *had* a voice mail. If he didn't, the back-up plan was to leave an anonymous tip on the Crime-Stoppers Hotline.

"Who's this?" the receptionist asked.

"It's, uh, Victor Watson."

I was thinking on the fly, taking Victor from <u>Victoria's Sweet Shoppe</u> across the street and the name of the bar—Watson's.

"I'll patch you through," she said, without hesitation.

Thank God, I thought to myself.

"This is Sheriff John Perembrooke. I'm either away from my desk or out in the field. Please leave a message or dial zero to return to the operator."

Here it was.

The time to speak was now.

"I have information on Donald Gallin." I took in a deep breath and continued. "2.8 miles east of Club Camber. 143 steps, south side of the road. Wax Murtle Tree."

I pressed the end call button and stopped the scrambler.

"Done," I said, wiping the devices down with soap and water.

I thought of Luke as I did that, remembering how he described cleaning off Donald Gallin's car. Wiping away any trace of his presence. I dried everything with paper towels and swiped the soap dispenser, faucets, and lock. I stepped out of the bathroom, wiping the doorknob down on both sides as I left.

I left the bar waiting for the door to open to slip myself out without touching anything—just as I did when I entered. I walked a few feet to the corner and dumped the phone in the trashcan. A few blocks later, I tossed the voice scrambler.

The streets were full of activity, cars, trucks, people everywhere, but I really didn't care. I was in my own mind. I actually thought I'd feel relief, but instead, I felt nothing.

Just numbness again.

I walked all the way back to Madison Square Garden and to 37th Street where the minivan was parked. I took the 59th Street Bridge to cross the East River, the same as I did on the trip in. No tickets, tolls, or cameras to catch me coming or going. But I don't remember if I stayed on the Long Island

Expressway or veered onto the Northern State Parkway as I made my way back to Nicole's.

What I do know is I slept until noon the next day, hoping the nothingness would dissolve.

It didn't.

Broomefield

Wednesday, January 10

On my way home from the airport, I picked up Elvis at The Cat Cottage, a hotel for cats that operated just outside of Boulder. It was a clever business—a converted house that had a lobby, a grooming spa, a jungle gym, and fifteen private rooms for "guests."

The hotel director, Dr. Rachel Zadrozny, came up with the idea when she retired from veterinary medicine. It was a way to move into her golden years and still be around the animals she loved. Zadrozny employed a staff of ten, mostly pre-med college students, who tended to each cat with the utmost of care.

"So, how'd my little guy do?"

"He was a delight," she said with a kind, wise smile. Zadrozny buzzed for one of the "bellhops" before talking with me again. "Got along with the other guests. Explored every nook and cranny. Ate heartily. Slept well."

"Sounds like he didn't miss me."

"Oh, every baby misses his mama."

Just then, a squeaky sound off in the distance caught my attention. It was a customized bell cart, with a pet cage made of brass piping. The lower bottom half was a shelf of deep, plush red carpet for belongings—just like the ones used in hotels.

I saw Elvis stretching across a velvet-tufted pillow. He looked so regal, narrowing his eyes and flapping his tail in rhythm with the turn of the wheels. As the afternoon sun gleamed against the polished brass of the carriage, I let out a long laugh.

"Oh, man. They'll be no living with him now."

"Well, Elvis *is* The King," the bellhop said.

"You know, back in my heyday, I used to have long, dark hair. Just like Priscilla—and that Ginger Alden," Zadrozny said, touching her powder-white pixie haircut.

"Back in my heyday, I had eighties mall hair. Nothing good about *that,*" I said.

The bellhop got Elvis' toys, food, and carrier from the lower shelves of the cart and set them on the lobby table. He opened a draw in the table and handed me a cellophane wrapped sachet.

"Organic catnip. We grow it here, mix in other essential oils, and package it ourselves," he said.

"Our mint on the pillow, cat style," Zadrozny said.

I placed my nose near the ribbon's knot and took in a whiff. "Mmm... Lemony."

"Lemon verbena mint, to be exact. My own recipe," the bellhop said.

"Hector aced medical botany," Zadrozny said.

"My best subject," he replied.

"Well, you guys have thought of everything. Makes me wish I was a cat."

"That's what we like to hear. Don't we, Hector?"

"Yup. Sure do."

Zadrozny opened the cage and took Elvis out. She stroked his black fur as Hector readied the pet carrier. Elvis scurried in without a sound.

"I hope you'll think of us again when you head out of town, Dr. Reese."

"I certainly will," I said, handing a tip to Hector.

"Have a good rest of the day now," Zadrozny said, walking away.

"Wait. What about the bill?" I asked.

"Oh, it's been paid in full already," Zadrozny said.

"No. That's not right. I didn't pay yet."

"You didn't?" She wrinkled her brow and walked behind the desk. "I thought you did."

Zadrozny went to the computer and moved the mouse with gentle sweeps of her hand.

"Lorraine did the transaction—she's out to lunch now, but it says here, *paid in full.*"

"Oh, that must have been my sister, Nicole's, doing. We do that sometimes—pay for things when the other is away."

"That's sweet."

"She's thoughtful like that," I said on my way out.

I pulled out my phone and dialed relay services as I walked to the car.

"This is operator 1806 at New York Relay. What number do you want to call?"

"I'd like to call 631-555-2080."

"I'll be off the line until the TTY user connects," she said, placing me on hold. "There's no one picking up. Would you like to leave a message?"

"Yes. Please say, *Hi Nic. It's Ali. Thanks for taking care of Elvis. That was such a surprise to come home to.*"

Boulder

Wednesday, January 10

Once I arrived home, I got Elvis settled back into the house and unpacked my things. It didn't take long before thoughts of Luke churned in my mind again.

I wondered how my phone call to Sheriff Perembrooke played out. Would it be considered real? Or a hoax? Would it be given high priority?

I bet they had to check it out, I thought to myself.

As my thoughts drifted, I walked into the kitchen to brew some tea. I reminded myself that it'd be risky to search for news updates online. I had no friends or family in Florida to call and chat with—no way to direct a conversation to the case.

While I was in New York, I thought about phoning one of the papers in Florida to verify if there was anything going on with the Gallin case. But I didn't because that wouldn't have been a smart move either. I'd have to let time take its course.

While the chamomile was steeping, I opened the curtains that were closed during my trip to New York. It snowed ten inches while I was gone, which covered the mountains in a veil of icy white. It was beautiful—and the view was breathtaking.

Stepping back from the window, I turned my attention to the computer. I sat down, turned it on, and waited for it to boot up. I clicked on the icon of my Yahoo homepage ready to check my email. But I saw it out of the corner of my eye. Down where the news of the day gets listed on the webpage.

It was the result of my call to Perembrooke.

<u>Anonymous Tip Uncovers Body of Missing Florida Man</u>

"They found him."

I moved the cursor over the link and nearly clicked it.

No, don't, I thought to myself. *Could be tracked.*

I sat back in my chair and considered what Perembrooke's discovery of Gallin's body meant for Luke. If it might free him from the anguish he expressed about leaving him there. I wondered about the work we did in the past. The symbolic and the literal meanings we covered in the analysis.

I wondered if he'd realize he let the last spider go.

I was quiet for some time before I returned to my thoughts. As I opened my eyes, I wondered if Luke sent me out to complete this last task not only to bring him relief and to offer closure to the Gallin family, but to allow me to know that in some small way he understood the point of it all.

That the hard thing to do and the right thing to do were one and the same.

Just as I was taking it all in, my cell phone rang.

"Hello?" I said, seeing on the caller ID that it was The Cat Cottage.

"Hi, Dr. Reese. This is Lorraine, from The Cat Cottage."

"Hello Lorraine."

"I was hoping to catch you before you called your sister."

"Oh, I already did. Why's that?"

"Well, Dr. Zadrozny told me about your conversation, and I didn't want you to find yourself in an awkward situation. You see, it wasn't your sister who paid the bill. It was a friend of yours."

"Friend?"

"Penny."

"Kenny?" I said, not recognizing the name.

"No, Dr. Reese. Penny. Penny Kingston."

I said nothing but felt a familiarity with the name. First, it started as a numb awareness, gnawing at my faulty recall.

"She said you might recognize her married name better." Lorraine shuffled papers before she spoke again. "Oh, here it is. Penny Ferro."

Every one of my senses dimmed. I felt myself disappear to a faraway place —like standing helplessly at the end of an ever-expanding hallway.

Oh God, why would Luke do this? What does this mean? I thought to myself.

I dropped the phone and stood for a moment, frozen in fear. I knew there'd come a time when he'd try to find me. I just didn't think it would happen this fast.

I bent down and picked up the phone. I heard Lorraine's muffled voice calling out. "Hello? Dr. Reese? Are you still there?"

"Sorry, I dropped the phone for a second."

"Oh good, I thought I lost you."

"Lorraine, when did the call come in?"

"Oh, there wasn't a call, Dr. Reese. She came in yesterday. Around four o'clock."

My mind couldn't make sense of it. "Did you say *she?*"

"Uh huh."

"In person?"

"Yes. Said you took care of her baby, and now she was going to take care of yours. Something like that."

"What?"

"She said you'd be surprised. Guess she was right."

I wasn't surprised. I was confused. I was terrified.

But as a shadow moved into the light by the front door, it all began to make sense.

"Lorraine..." I said.

"Yes?"

"I have to go now. Penny Ferro is at my door."

Boulder

Wednesday, January 10

L uke had dark blue eyes and facial features like his mother.
And as Penny Ferro stood on the landing by the front storm door, I
witnessed the same impatient traits they shared. The disdainful gaze.
The hand tapping. The heavy breathing.

"You really need someone to clear your walkway while you're gone," she
said.

"Yes, I guess I should."

"Good thing my driver had a shovel," she remarked with a head nod.

I looked beyond the front porch and saw a thick-set man in a bank of
snow. His coat whipped in the wind as he cleared a path through the knee-
high layers.

Behind him chugged a black stretch limousine. I watched its windshield
wipers flap across the glass like a metronome on double time. I couldn't help
but notice how my heartbeat matched its rhythmic strokes.

"A Cadillac?" I asked, recognizing the chassis.

"Yes. Only car I ever step into." Ferro moved inside the house and pulled
a self-satisfied smile across her lips. "I enjoy driving around in a well-appointed
vehicle. It's a splendid way to get to see things. Get to know people."

I looked at her and then to the car outside. I instantly realized that Luke
hadn't been in the Black Cadillac that followed me back in New York.

It was Penny Ferro.

My mouth hung open as I connected the dots.

"You're surprised," Ferro said, fascinated by my discomfort.

I said nothing.

Ferro brushed the wet snow from her white fur coat in long strokes, sending heavy droplets of water to the floor without concern. Then she removed her gloves, pulling off each finger with a theatrical tug.

I never met Penny Ferro, but I knew her. From the way she carried herself and who she revealed herself to be. Ferro was a narcissist, a malignant narcissist—and a psychopath in her own right.

But she was also a cliché.

Her behaviors were right out of an abnormal psychology book. Typical in every way. Classic in their breadth and depth.

I realized to beat her at her own game, I needed to stop reacting emotionally. The way to get the upper hand now was to see her through an analytic lens. If I approached things clinically, I'd see her pathology, and maybe, find my balance.

I struggled to calm myself. I tried slowing my thoughts and getting control of my racing heart, but all I did was stumble on my words when I finally spoke.

"H-how did you…?" I asked.

"Now, come on, Alicia. Spit it out," Ferro said, dipping her chin.

Stay focused. Don't lose it, I told myself. *She's trying to intimidate you. Don't let that happen. Don't fall into the trap of her condescending manner by getting angry. That's what she wants.*

"You must've spent a lot of money on your disappearing act," I finally said.

"Oh yes. And a lot of time planning once I made the decision."

"And when did you make that?" I asked.

"Some years ago," she replied with a smile.

"What was the final straw?"

"I know you'd like to hear that it was something really big. Or a specific event. But it was just a simple realization."

Ferro licked her lips and waited for the right moment to continue. Like a musical conductor, she set the tone as well as the downbeat.

"If I wasn't going to be everything to them, I'd rather be nothing to them. I'd go away. And when someone dies, it's almost like their memory intensifies, haunting you. Wouldn't you say that's the case for you, Alicia?"

I ignored her question. Instead, I asked, "So, you leave behind everything and everyone you know? Just like that?"

"*Just like that*," she said repeating my words.

"Even your grandchildren?" I asked.

"Come on. You're smart enough to realize that I don't give them a second thought."

It was true. I knew that now. But on another level, I couldn't believe the magnitude of her narcissism. How cold she truly was. I was beginning to understand what kind of mother she must have really been to Luke. I stood quiet and still, realizing she lived entirely *by* and *for* herself.

Distracted by my silence, Ferro sought her reflection in a nearby mirror. She noticed her hair was untidy and windblown. She fixed it with a few sweeps of her manicured hands—tending to each strand, smoothing it into place. And just like Narcissus in Greek mythology, Ferro got lost in her own reflection. Only the sound of Elvis bounding into the room broke the mirror's spell.

"It took a few years to funnel money to an offshore account in the Cayman's. Then there was enticing the emergency room doctor and the medical examiner."

I nodded, examining her every move.

"Oh, and the funeral director," Ferro said as Elvis nosed his way toward her. "Everyone has a price."

"They do?"

"Of course. Don't you ever wonder what yours is?"

"No amount of money in the world could give me what I want."

"Yes. Your dead husband." Ferro arched her brows. "Isn't there more you want?"

I wanted Ryan here. But I also wanted intangible things Ferro would never understand. Integrity. Self-respect.

"No. Nothing more," I said.

"You know what your problem is?" she asked.

"I have many problems. And I know what they *all* are, thank you."

Elvis began lapping up the little pools of water around Ferro's feet. Before he could finish, she bent over and picked him up. "I had a beautiful cat once. Named her Penny."

Ferro stopped talking to delight in touching Elvis. She raked her fingers through his fur, causing him to purr loudly. Elvis thanked her by nuzzling her neck.

I wanted to yank him away but didn't.

Stay calm, Alicia.

"Your cat's name is Elvis? Isn't that right?" she asked, still stroking Elvis.

"Yes," I said, irritated she knew so much about me.

"Funny how we name our pets after things we love." Ferro kept petting Elvis but returned her gaze toward me. "So, you must be an Elvis Presley fan."

"You could say that."

"Well, I named my cat after what I loved most in this world."

"Yourself?"

"No." Ferro laughed and looked away. "Money. Her full name was Every Little Penny."

"Interesting," I said.

"You know, that little shit son of mine drowned her in the pool. He never admitted it, but I knew it was him."

It never occurred to me that Luke's mother knew what happened to Penny. I thought her arrogance would've blunted the ability to see beyond her own self. I was learning not to underestimate her.

"Oh, he didn't tell you?" she asked.

"No." I said, lying.

Ferro stopped petting Elvis and locked her eyes back onto mine. I felt them trace an icy outline as they moved along my face. "Mmmm... I think he *did* tell you," she said, studying me.

"It doesn't really matter now. Does it?"

"But it does help explain things," she said.

"Like what?"

"Well, most serial killers start off murdering animals, don't they?"

I said nothing, remaining still, but I was overwhelmed with a flood of thoughts. I tried to ground myself by focusing on my breathing as Penny Ferro began talking about herself.

"I inherited everything from my father, but that wasn't my true destiny," she said. "I had younger brothers, who, of course, were groomed to take over the business. I was the debutante daughter trained for other things. The best schools to learn English, French, and Latin. How to cook, sew, dance. Even how to arrange flowers. Diction and dress, poise and posture. You know, groomed to be someone's wife. But that wasn't for me. I knew I had to change things."

Ferro paused as if to create more tension than there already was in the air.

"My middle brother, Dean, was in a terrible accident skiing in Vermont when he was 22. The binding in his left ski snapped off and he lost control. Poor thing hit a tree and rolled down the hillside. Suffered a life-changing head injury."

My eyes widened.

"Oh, he isn't dead," Ferro replied. "I could never, ever do that. Dean's been in a wheelchair since I rigged the binding. But, he's well taken care of. Even to this day."

My lips trembled as my mouth fell open. *Oh my god. She just told me it wasn't an accident.*

"My younger brother, Andrew—that was easier. A running supply of liquor got him hooked in high school—and later in and out of treatment centers," Ferro continued. "By the time he graduated college, he was a full time drunk."

Holy hell, I thought to myself. *She's soulless.*

"When everyone lectured that he had a disease, I told him he didn't."

Ferro eased her stare and looked back at Elvis. She began running her fingers again through his fur.

"And when mother and father forbid Andrew to live in the house if he was drinking, I'd visit him wherever he was and bring him whatever he wanted. Vodka. Tequila. Beer."

"So thoughtful of you," I said, finally finding the strength to speak again.

"Yes. I was a *very* thoughtful enabler," she replied.

All of a sudden, Ferro stopped talking. And moving. She looked at me stone-faced, her eyes narrowing as she spoke again.

"I never killed anyone to get what I needed. But the thought crossed my mind many, many times," she said. "To know Lucas did–well, maybe I wrote the boy off too soon."

I suddenly thought of the psychological theory, *intergenerational trauma,* which explains how some children inherit their parent's pains, traumas, and wishes. How Penny Ferro's unspoken desires for murder and annihilation found a way into Luke's mind, body, and soul. That Luke, himself, was groomed to become a violent offender by his own mother's unfulfilled urges.

I was back into a full-clinical mode of thinking–the place where I was always strong and confident. I was no longer overwhelmed by Penny Ferro's sudden presence.

"What is it you want?" I asked finally.

"You know, I have always been the most important woman in Lucas' life. He may have hated me, but hate is a form of devotion. When I *died*, he really fell apart. I had my people keep an eye on all of my sons, and to my delight, I heard that he was a mess."

"What does this have to do with me?" I asked her.

"Well, he has been to therapy before, but it was always a fickle endeavor. When I was informed that he'd been visiting your home, I just *had* to find out more about my competition."

"Your competition?"

"Why yes, dear. His hate for me was an obsession, and it seems that you became his new obsession."

She's right. Luke is obsessed with me, I thought to myself. I was about to speak again, but Ferro waved me off with her hand.

"Look, I was following the news stories about Lucas. Hoping for a long trial. But he got locked away without one, and I was so disappointed. I was hoping you'd tell me what happened—the details I can't read about in the press."

"I really don't know."

"Your mommy's lying," Ferro said looking at Elvis.

"And how do you know that?"

"I know your mommy went to see Lucas at the jail in East Meadow—and she threatened him with something. There was a big fight there, Elvis. Didn't she tell you?"

"Your payroll is bigger than you let on."

Ferro looked at me with a sidelong glance. "The guards didn't hear the specifics though," she said.

"Can't say I'm sorry to hear that," I replied.

"That job is so dreadful. I don't know how they do it, quite frankly. It's even worse in Ossining."

Her reach is immense and her poison is everywhere, I said to myself.

"Sheridan wasn't his first kill, I imagine," Ferro continued. "I've had my suspicions over the years that there were others. I just want to know more."

I tried to stay calm but couldn't hold things together anymore. My anger boiled out of control. "Listen, Penny or whatever you're calling yourself now, I'm not telling you a goddam thing."

"It'd be nice to know Lucas' real story. That's all. No need to be so defensive." Ferro released Elvis gently to the floor and watched as he trotted away to his bed.

Get out! Get out! Get out of my house! I wanted to scream aloud, but I refused to let Ferro see how raw and angry I was. Instead, I moved toward the storm door and pressed the handle down.

"It's time for you to leave," I said.

"So, my money can't entice you to tell me what happened?"

"That's right."

"And you won't share anything out of the goodness of your heart either?"

"Uh, no."

Ferro tried one more time. "I've traveled so far to come and see you."

"Please go."

"Well, then, I'll just thank you and..."

"And be on your way," I said, finishing the sentence.

"Yes," Ferro said, wanting to have the last word.

I watched as she knotted her silk scarf around her neck and slipped the gloves back on.

"I'm untraceable," Ferro said over her shoulder as she passed by.

"I'm sure you are."

"The payment to The Cat Cottage was an American Express wire transfer. The limousine was paid for in cash. And by the time you call someone to follow me, I'll be long gone."

"Yes, I know," I said, realizing the scope of her intellect and power.

"He isn't done with you, Alicia."

"What?" I asked.

"*You* are his new obsession. And even though he gave you a little punch in the face, he hasn't written you off. So when you talk with Lucas, which I'm *sure* you *will*, tell him, I'm so very proud of him."

As the door closed, Elvis jumped up and pressed his front paws on the glass. He made little patches of steamy circles with each meow he cried, calling after her.

Together we watched as Penelope Kingston Ferro commanded the driver to open the car door with a swing of her arm and then made him wait as she opened her purse. I cringed as he stood in pathetic subservience, waiting in the bitter cold as Ferro brought out her thorns.

She lingered a moment, took out a compact, and powdered her nose—something she could've done after she entered the limousine.

But where's the amusement in that?

Make me mad, you'll pay in spades.

I thought about how we're born into this world. How nature, our genetic wiring, predispositions and tendencies—and nurture, how we're loved and cared for, shape who we are.

My heart sank realizing when I stood in front of Penny Ferro, it was nature and nurture at its worst.

Luke never had a chance, I thought to myself as I pressed the video button on my cell phone off.

Tenth Session

Friday, January 12

❝I wasn't expecting anyone today," Luke said.

"You didn't get my letter?"

"No." Luke closed his eyes slowly and spoke again. "When did you send it?"

"Wednesday. Overnight express."

"Well, the mail's slow here. I'll probably get it tomorrow."

"I wanted you to know I was coming."

"It's no big deal."

I changed the course of Luke's life in so many ways. Now I was going to pull the rug out from under him again. My letter would have made our meeting so much easier. He would've been prepared for things. Worry swelled within me. I stared at him blankly, not knowing where to start.

"Really, Dr. Reese, it's fine."

He seems okay, Alicia. Keep going, I said to myself.

I turned away for a moment to settle my nerves by taking in a deep breath. What a sudden contradiction it was as Luke watched me work the anxiety-reducing technique.

"What's going on?" Luke asked.

"This place—it's tough."

"You get used to it," he said with a sway of his hand.

Luke's words had a slight slur to them, and now I noticed how unsteady his movements were. He looked slightly heavier than when I last saw him.

"Got me on brake fluid," he said, sensing my awareness.

"Which one?"

"Depakote. It helps."

"Well, that's good," I offered, not really knowing what else to say.

"I don't get visitors much. It's good getting out of the cell block."

"Your family doesn't come?"

"My brothers do—every now and then."

"What about your father?"

"If it's on his way to something," he scoffed. "Some things don't change."

"That's disappointing to hear."

Luke said nothing and drifted away. I followed his eyes as he glanced at the inmates. The visiting room was full and busy with activity. But it was easy to see the broken lives. The fractured families. It was a hard sight to take in. Even harder to be part of it.

"I wanted to tell you that what you did—in your letter for Perembrooke—it all worked out," I said, starting the conversation again.

"I know. Saw it online."

"That was really something, Luke."

"Well, you spend a lot of time thinking here. It gets to you."

I nodded quietly, feeling responsible for a great deal of his misery. "Has it helped?"

"You mean taking away the panic attacks?"

"Yes."

"They stopped the minute I mailed it."

"I'm glad about that."

"I knew you'd take care of things." Luke blinked, his eyes heavy lidded from the medication. "Is that why you came here? To tell me that?"

"Well, yes. But, I have something else to tell you."

"What?"

"It's—it's about your mother."

"What about her?"

"This is going to be hard to hear." I leaned closer to him. "She's not dead."

Every aspect of his face stretched out in shock. His eyes widened, his cheeks flushed, and his mouth dropped open. "She's not?"

"No. She's alive, Luke."

"Wait, what?"

"She came to see me in Colorado. She showed up at my house."

Luke became motionless, connected to me, but barely. There was so much more to say, but I waited for him to be ready.

After a while, he drifted back.

"Luke, I have something to show you."

I pulled an envelope from my pocket. The movement caught the eye of a nearby corrections officer. "Whattya got there?" he said, grabbing my arm.

"Just some photos."

The officer was a muscular man with a timeworn face. He was well into his fifties and reminded me of a tugboat—on the small side, but strong and powerful. He released my arm, took the envelope in his hands, and looked at its contents.

"You're *not* supposed to give anything directly to the inmate."

"Yes, I'm sorry. I forgot."

"Got anything else on you?" He glared at me as he rifled through the pictures.

"No. Just that."

"Good," the officer said. "Here, take this Ferro."

Luke didn't move and didn't even look up.

The corrections officer snapped his fingers in front of Luke's face.

"Can you just put them in front of him?" I asked.

"Why?"

"So he can look at them when he's ready."

"What's to get ready for? It's just some lady in a full-on fur coat."

"Is it white?" Luke turned his head toward the officer and stared.

"It's white," he said. "Like fucking snow."

Luke took the envelope and waited for the officer to leave. He pressed his lips together and jutted his chin out. With a grim-set look on his face, he opened it and looked at the pictures. He stared at the first one. Then the second. His eyes glossed over by the time he reached the third one.

"Y'know, my brothers said they never saw her in the hospital."

"Not even to identify the body?"

"Nope."

"Who did then?"

"My father. Through some window in the morgue there."

"Did *you* see her after the accident?"

"No. When I came up the next day she was already cremated."

"Your mother had everything play out quickly."

"Well, everything *did* happen fast," Luke said.

"She was counting on the chaos."

"The art of distraction. Her specialty."

Luke remained quiet for a while. And so did I, sitting back in the metal chair. I waited for him to speak again.

"So, who's in her pocket?" Luke asked.

"The hospital staff, the M.E., and the funeral director." I lowered my voice to a hush. "And the guards."

We both stopped talking and looked at the team of corrections officers that lined the room's perimeter.

"She knew about our fight in East Meadow. She wanted to know what I had on you. Why there wasn't a trial."

Luke clenched his fists. The blood rushed away from his knuckles, leaving them a mottled white color. "Did you tell her about Gallin?"

"No, why would I?"

Weakened and devastated, he slumped forward.

"How'd she find you?" he asked after a few moments.

"Not exactly sure. She showed up at my door two days ago."

"She wasn't really worried about me, right?"

I nodded.

"Yeah, well, that's not a surprise. She was just sniffing around."

"Well, I didn't tell her anything."

"Where'd these pictures come from?"

"My cell. Your mother didn't know I used it to record her visit."

"Smart."

"It was luck, really. I was on the phone when she showed up."

"Still, that's a smooth move. And it'll chap her ass when she finds out."

I looked away and smiled, realizing he was right.

"Does anyone else know?" he asked.

"You mean, your brothers? Your father?"

"Yeah."

"No. I came here first. I couldn't bring my phone in for you to see the video. But I can send them a copy if you want."

"Yeah, they should know. Could you get in touch with them for me?"

"Sure. I'll reach out."

"Uncle Dean and Uncle Drew – her brothers. They should know too."

Luke mentioning his uncles made me wonder if I should tell him what his mother did to them.

Would it be too much to add at this time?

Would it send him over the edge?

As I reflected further, a painful awareness surfaced in Luke's face.

"You know, she never wanted me," he said.

"Your mother?"

"Yeah. She was almost six months when she realized she was pregnant."

"Six months? How could she *not* know she was pregnant?"

Luke hiked his shoulders. "She tried to get an abortion, but, you know, she was too far along. No doctor would touch her."

"How do you know this?"

"She told me. Many times, in fact. Right up till the day she died. Or should I say, disappeared."

"Jesus," I said, shrinking back in my seat.

"Once, my father heard her telling me, and he blew a fucking gasket. Said he didn't want anything to do with her anymore."

"How old were you when this happened?"

"Five. Maybe six," Luke said, rubbing his brows with the heels of his hands.

I struggled to find something to say but found my thoughts swimming in analytic phrases like *Dead Mother* and *Black Milk*. Terms that characterized severe psychological dysfunction between a mother and a child.

Before I let my associations deepen, Luke rose from his chair. He took one photo from the set on the table, waved it in the air for the nearest corrections officer to see, and tucked it in his jumpsuit pocket.

There was so much more I wanted to talk to him about, but Luke walked away from me.

And never looked back to say goodbye.

Maybe Mommy Dearest was wrong. Maybe this is the end, and now we can both move on, I thought to myself.

I gathered the leftover photos and went to the rented locker in the visiting area to retrieve my belongings. I looked at the rugged cliffs of the Palisades and the frosty banks of the Hudson River as I left the dreary prison grounds. I wondered how such beauty and sorrow could exist simultaneously in this place called Ossining.

I wiped my eyes, straining not to cry as I drove north on Hunter to Secor. But by the time I turned South on the Taconic Parkway, my eyes spilled over.

I thought about Luke being despised by his own mother even before he was born.

That she was as evil as she was damaged.

And that she offered him nothing but the emotional leftovers of bones and crumbs, of gristle and rind.

How could her bitterness and hate do anything other than turn his heart to stone?

There was only one thing Luke could be.

Deformed.

The realization of it all hit me hard. My fingers wilted around the steering wheel, and my body, stiff and tense moments ago, was heavy from the force of gravity. Weary, broken, and utterly alone, I was on the brink of collapse. I felt the nothingness of despair closing in. Crushing me.

I gathered all my strength and jammed the brakes, screeching the car to the shoulder of the highway. I hauled the drive shaft into park and snapped on the emergency lights.

Everything became cold.

Especially my hands. They felt like ice. I pulled them closer and tried to warm them with my breath. I shook my palms and fingers hard and let them fall limply in my lap.

For a moment, I regarded them.

My hands didn't just reach, touch, feel, and grasp. My hands housed a voice.

I held them open and positioned them flat-palmed near my shoulders— just ahead of my body. I pushed them outward. Over and over and over again.

The sign meant many things.

Go on.

Forward.

Future.

I grabbed the cell phone from my handbag and reached for the business card of Dr. Prader's colleague in Colorado, Dr. Eric Bibleaux.

I thought about the twists and turns of fate and the secrets I'd hidden for so long as I pressed the numbers.

I closed my eyes and imagined sitting in the waiting room in a chair nearest to the exit.

How the light would slowly filter in from the other room as Dr. Bibleaux opened the door. I thought about the last moment of the unknown, where two strangers meet and a life story begins.

And as the phone rang, I hit the hands-free Bluetooth button in the Saab, ready to make the call.

And merged back onto the highway.

Deborah Serani is an award-winning author and psychologist who has been in practice for thirty years. She is also a professor at Adelphi University and is a go-to media expert for psychological issues. Her interviews can be found in *Newsday*, *Psychology Today*, *The Chicago Tribune*, *The New York Times*, *The Associated Press*, and affiliate radio programs at CBS and NPR, among others. Dr. Serani has also been a technical advisor for the NBC television show, *Law & Order: Special Victims Unit*. The character Judge D. Serani was named after her.

CPSIA information can be obtained
at www.ICGtesting.com
Printed in the USA
LVHW111740300120
645335LV00007B/984